SINFUL MONSTERS

UNLEASHED BY THE DRAGON - A DARK MONSTER ROMANCE NOVELLA

EDITH SADA

Sinful Monsters - Unleashed By The Dragon (Book One in Monsters Of Scorched Earth)
Copyright © 2022 by Edith Sada

All rights reserved. No part of this book may be reproduced or transmitted in any form, including electronic or mechanical, without written permission from the publisher, except in the case of brief quotations embodied in critical articles or reviews.
This is a work of fiction. Names, characters, businesses, places, events, and incidents are either the products of the author's imagination or used in a fictitious manner. Any resemblance to actual persons, living or dead, or actual events is purely coincidental.
This book is licensed for your personal enjoyment only. This book may not be re-sold or given away to other people. If you would like to share this book with another person, please purchase an additional copy for each person you share it with. If you are reading this book and did not purchase it, or it was not purchased for your use only, then you should return it to the seller and purchase your own copy. Thank you for respecting the author's work.

Trigger Warning

Please note this is a dark monster romance and not suitable for readers who have triggers. Content included can be hard to read and only recommended for readers who like dark monster romance.

ABOUT THE AUTHOR

Edith publishes her first in the dark monster romance genre with this book.
What started as a challenge quickly turned into one of her favorite projects.
Let this be a beginning for Edith as it is for the "heroes" of the story.
Enjoy Scorched Earth.

**Release Day Alerts, Sneak Peek
and Newsletter**
To be first to know about upcoming releases, please join Edith's Newsletter.
https://subscribepage.io/edithsada_newsletter

Author Edith Sada
An der Kirche 9
06571 Roßleben-Wiehe OT Roßleben
edithsada.author@gmail.com

„Change can be scary,
but you know what's scarier?
Allowing fear to stop you
from growing,
evolving, and progressing."
Mandy Hale

CHAPTER ONE

I PLUNGED MY HEAVY HEARTBEAT INTO THE HIGH SEAS OF MY consciousness, gasping for air as I loathed the end of my workday that lay ahead, glittering with the muddy promise of a safe haven.

For the next long promising eight hours I would be safe from my own thoughts and protected from the nightmares that would claw at my sleeping form.

If only it were true.

The warmth from the hanging lamps laving the turquoise walls of the men's locker room failed to loosen the goosebumps that spidered down my back.

Too close the upcoming trial that held a tether around my thoughts. I struggled for the freedom that was already dangling within my reach. My thoughts already on the adventures that would lie ahead.

I scanned each of the changing booths and collected the wet dog-smelling towels the customers had dropped on the floor and laid them into the already overflowing basket in front of me, wishing that someone would pick me up from the floor and caress me.

Not possible.

I was ready to leave this dammed bath house for good.

It wasn't enough for me anymore, my future lingering right around the corner. I wanted to get things started.

But the balance in my bank account wasn't high enough. *Yet.*

I just needed to wait until after the trial.

That's when huge amounts of money would flood my balance.

Still, I couldn't be certain, my only reason to linger.

The suppressed air in my lungs escaped in a quiver, disturbing the quietness around me.

Gray mountains of towels lulled me in and had never failed as my rope, keeping me bound to the shore.

Sunken in myself my hearing was hushed and made it almost impossible to hear the knock behind me.

Distant, deep, deep down.

It seemed like small fish nudging my feet. But to me it was the shark at my legs with an open mouth ready to swallow.

My job was hanging on a silken thread after I was late to work again.

After it took me forever to change.

I knew the consequences.

Still, I couldn't bring myself to it.

Gazing in the mirror, my skin looked sallow from teeth of past horrors gnawing at me. My brittle hair lackluster like my eyes. My shape starved, no mellow flesh on me.

I tore my eyes away, could not bear the person staring at me. Barely alive, appraising, waiting in greed.

I was a greedy person.

I fiddled my cotton top down and my shorts up, gaining no inch from my exposed belly.

A rumble shook the room and the changing room door hit the wall.

My face remained a silken mask, gazing at the intruder through the mirror.

"Your appearance will not magically change the longer you stare at this poor thing of yours, Kaida."

My boss.

The owner of the Relax, Bathe and Unwind bathhouse, also called the RBU. The interior looked as if the previous owner forgot to take the image of the whorehouse with him. Big, bigger, swanky. But it was a new building. He thought he owned the best bathhouse in town.

I would show him how to do it properly.

His presence alone made it impossible for women to relax, catering exclusively to men.

Rumlar Wolf.

A Hellhound.

He had no resemblance to the Hellhounds from folklore.

Not that I'd been there when they lived, just my imagination.

Rumlar clicked his tongue.

My eyes narrowed into slits.

His yellow eyes, compressed in his usual disgust whenever he saw me, now roaming around my figure, stood in contrast to the dense red fur that infested his whole body.

Even he wasn't sure if I should wear this uniform.

Towering behind me, his meaty body was ready to undermine at the first sight of fear.

I knew better.

I wouldn't let him off with his behavior.

We played the same ridiculous game every day.

Who stares the other into the ground and makes them speak first.

He thought I liked him, that we had a decent relationship.

Hell no.

3

Just pretending.

A headache rolled up behind my eyes.

He always gave in first.

One, Two, Three—

"Take the laundry basket to the back and go to cabin three. A customer wants an infusion."

I flicked my hair and marched towards the door.

His bulky arm shot forward stopping me in my tracks.

"Don't forget to smile." His voice oozed out of him like his foul breath.

I forced the corners of my mouth upwards.

His face told me everything. I had failed.

"Not like this. You're scarier than some of our guests."

I smacked his shoulder and drew a big boy grin from him.

The easiest task.

"Fuck you!" I said.

CHAPTER TWO

I ENTERED CABIN THREE, ONE OF OUR STEAM BATHS, LEAVING the door open.

Bright haze danced over my vision, obscuring most of the room.

I bowed in the direction where the customer should rest, doing my best to be polite and leave my annoyance behind.

The lingering scent of hibiscus rose to my nose, mingled with the masculine odor of old ship planks weathered by the rough sea.

Everything screamed in relaxation.

Next to the massive heater, enclosed in huge deep blue and black stones, I set the wooden sauna bucket down. The velvet texture of the stones called for me. To touch them just once.

I abandoned the thought when a cough pulled me out of it.

Clicking my tongue I said: "Welcome to the RBU. Have you been in the sauna for at least 10 minutes?"

A snort was his only response.

Great.

"Very well. Let me start the infusion. Sit back, relax, bathe and unwind."

The clientele was not inferior to Rumlar. Vigorous, dominant men sitting in positions of privilege, wanting to be served by lowly women.

I didn't know what he was. But the size of the booth told me he was a monster. The specialty of the RBU. Sauna and massage for the big boys.

Literally.

The cabins were set in wood that was salvaged from shipwrecks. Excellent for indoor climate. Very rare to get and the essence and warmth they dispersed, heavenly. The benches, however, were made of new pine wood to avoid splinters.

I envied Rumlar.

Beads of sweat tickled my scalp, pooling at my nape.

Right now, I thanked Rumlar for the wardrobe he forced us to wear.

It was warm.

Very warm.

I fished for the aroma bottles in my pocket. Preparing the water was the first step.

Mellow Lavender and Abyss Lovage, the ones for today.

A gift from above and probably the last for today that of all things my two favorites were chosen.

The girl that showed up early got to decide. Thus, the smell of these aromas followed one around the bathhouse like seagulls observing food.

I dripped one entire pipet of each into the lukewarm water of the bucket and whirled with the wooden trowel until they were joined.

The rising smell draped me in a robe of tender sun rays on a scorching summer day at the beach, kissing my senses, calming me.

Snatching the towel from my shoulder, I swirled fresh air in, enough for the infusion to work its magic.

The room shrunk as I closed the door with a soft thud, drowning the lounge music.

Leaving me with the client's steady breathing and my own. Which had accelerated.

Needle pricks stretched over my back, tingling my insides, nudging me to continue.

My neck tightened, and the headache knocked in greatest force behind my forehead.

I grabbed one full trowel of water and dribbled it over the oven.

Searing and cracking.

The temperature climbed, like the sun pushing past the clouds, heating exposed skin.

As instructed, I waited a minute between each added ladle before finishing with three in total.

Again, I snatched my towel and rotated it high above me.

Done, ready for the customer to enjoy the next 30 minutes—

"Can you pour another two ladles?"

A bitter tinge coated my tongue.

"Sorry, only three trowels per infusion!"

A blizzard dashed through my veins, settling in my gut, dehydrating the relief that had settled.

I thrust my hands into my hips, ready to pull his head out of his ass. "When—"

"Look, in case it escaped your notice, which I'm certain it did..." His voice barely a mumble but rich as a ripe fruit. "I'm alone, which is beside the point. Furthermore I rented this place. And let me explain it slow. I want the service I was promised."

My eyes bulged.

I must have misheard.

He had not dared to call me stupid.

"Are you going to move or should I hail your boss?" He said, putting further pressure on my head.

I whirled around. The man's finger was on the request button, the direct connection to Rumlar.

My heart shot into my stomach.

His legs opened wide, the delicate part that lay between his hips covered by a white cotton towel. His rib cage swelled and sank with solid breaths, scattering the light over his frame and highlighting a dozen shiny scales.

No man.

I draught in a breath.

He lowered his muscular arm and his forest green eyes drew me in.

My body went limp and my hands dropped to the side.

Every thought vanished from my brain and I stared at him, reclined on the bench.

I devoured every part of his tan, naked skin. White glowing veins snaked underneath every inch. The defined muscles on his arms and legs etched with eagerness and power. He looked as if he'd appeared straight from a fairy tale with long black hair surpassing defined shoulders and scales, like the ones from a dragon, scattered in clusters all over his body.

He leaned in, his hand now resting on his knee.

His gaze held me hostage.

One of his irises was shaped like that of a snake, swirling in lazy circles of yellow and green.

My breathing quickened. My mind raced with the possibilities... what he was.

A Drakon.

Every inch of my being struck with awareness.

I'd never seen one since I lived in the city, merely heard stories.

8

They had to be feared.

The flick of his tongue echoed from the wooden panels.

His eyebrow above the snake eye propped into his hairline.

My throat bobbed. I tried to mouth words. Any kind of them. I wet my lips and pushed past my shock, my voice wobbly. "Sure..."

I couldn't afford another warning from Rumlar right now.

"Simple." he said.

Turning away from him, I loaded another trowel, adding it on to the heater.

The hissing in sync with my thundering heartbeat, from the unknown, the hatred that he as a being was to me.

Sweat licked down my spine.

I didn't know if it was from the added steam. The duration in this room or the burning for this guy.

He leaned back, which caught my attention, his lush eyes narrowing as my breasts moved beneath my cotton top. A scorching intenseness drenched his stare, forcing my body to squirm. "What do you think you're doing?" I said.

Licking his bottom lip, left in greed, his gaze went down, roaming from head to toe.

Slowly, carefully, so eagerly, it felt like a violation and seduction all at once.

He feasted on me.

The glow of the snaking veins underneath his skin intensified. Clenching his fists, the muscles in his arms ripped and tugged. Large hands, the tips of each finger ending in lethal claws.

The smell of citrus and mountain dew shoved past the bouquet from the water, leashing my throat.

My cheeks reddened, the heat slumped past my bellybutton.

He chuckled, which made his Adam's apple quiver. "I'm taking the same thing you took from me. So we'll be even."

His lips rolled up in a smug grin, his eyes gleaming.

"What..." I slid my gaze down my body and met my underwear peeking through my clothes. I yanked my arms in front of my breasts. "Pervert!" This lousy pig, no decency in his butt. "Let me make this real clear. I wasn't fixated on you." I grinned and swallowed the worry of what would come later.

He sniffed the air. "Ha, then tell me why I can sniff your a—"

I drowned his remark in the hiss that echoed off the walls by slapping a ladle of water on the radiator, accidentally flinging hot drops of water on my arm, burning me.

I groaned. "Shit."

The trowel fell, bouncing off the floor and landing in front of the Drakon.

But he was already next to me. His massive palm shot forward and grabbed my injured arm.

He towered over me.

I flinched in pain.

CHAPTER THREE

I FLOPPED ON THE CHAIR BEHIND THE RECEPTION COUNTER, separated through a layer of glass from the spa section.

The skin under my bandage itched and increased my urge to rage further.

Light danced in orange and yellow streaks over the plush sofas of the waiting zone, placed on thick carpeting, attempting to make the stay at the RBU wholesome. Despite, no one was relaxing there on an early Tuesday morning.

The spa area was also empty. A cacophony tiled in baby blue from top to bottom, with a vast floor deep tub to cool down and unwind after the treatments in the middle. The few clients were either in the steam baths or massage rooms.

The air temperature compared to the steam bath was rather fresh, air whooshing through the vents, battling the heat in my system. It suffocated me, stripping my abominable thoughts, and rinsed away the fading dregs of debilitating anger.

I loosened my grip on the deflating feeling.

On my way back, I'd faced a lecture from Rumlar. Unaware of what had happened, his temper slapped me in the face for my entitlement to take an hour's break. If only he knew I had to change my clothes and bandage my arm because one of his customers overstepped.

Growing a lump of magma in the pit of my stomach.

Why had this Drakon needed it so hot, anyway?

Why had he threatened me? Sure, to him I was the tool to work his desires. Bringing him satisfaction over my well-being.

Nestling at the edges of the gauze, I pondered.

I despised myself.

And my stupid body reacting because of his sight. The image of his claws scratching over me crept into my thoughts. His wide neck protruded from his skull down into his massive frame. I just got a glimpse of his entire figure, but I would say he was at least 7.1 feet. Speckled with crystal scales, reflected with the colors of the setting sea. His pectoral muscle, carved from stone under his folded arms, begged for a touch. Narrow hips wrapped in smooth cotton touching his...

My breathing poured out of my gaping mouth in insufficient ripples that broke on the shore.

The slag in my belly liquefied further into lava and surged through my body, its center of gravity shifting further down.

A slight pulse of shame clenched my core and woke feelings I hadn't known before.

Never had my clothes gone see-through. I cursed these clothes even more.

And I cursed him for making me tremble.

Stupid, stupid, stupid.

I slammed my hand on the counter.

A tall figure appeared in my vision. I spun my head around, picking up the Drakon staring at me across the spa area.

He must have noticed my outburst, and I hated him more.

The towel that clung to his rigid, flawless body flew to the floor.

My jaw dropped, unable to hide the reaction to this ass.

And what an ass.

The lava inside me sparked in delight, creeping into my thighs, torching everything in its path.

My fingers twitched. I would love to claw my fingers into this magnificent specimen. But the most exciting part wasn't his peach but the long tail sticking out of his skin at the end of his back and above his buttocks, which I hadn't noticed before.

His tail jerked, hitting the wet tiles.

I dragged my gaze up.

Aware that he had my absolute attention, a sinful smile tugged at his plump lips.

Eyes piercing right through me.

Damn.

He strode into the pool. Spellbound I watched every stroke of the muscles in his ass clench and release.

The water curled away from him, evaporating into steam.

He dove, illuminating the water in pure white with tinges of purple and turquoise.

Amazing.

Fate had somehow read my hidden fantasies and woven together every piece that I found worthwhile in the male sex, amping it up on the design, fabricating something inherently spotless, all while hiding the decay deep inside. Layer over layer, tricking the eye.

His personality I already found horrendous.

When he'd talked down to me, a storm of loathing had flared in me.

His bygone, blizzard baritone oozed with blackness. It'd reached inside me and left a slick residue on my insides.

I realized what he was besides a monster.

I would not be stupid.

He was not a simple man.

This was someone I should never trust or let my guard slip.

He was a hunter, in a world rich of prey to his liking.

The pretty looking scales disguised the viciousness within and I had only caught a glimpse.

Unfortunately, I knew almost nothing about the various guests we welcomed to our bathhouse.

Until my family had moved to Alrade, I'd experienced nothing else except humans like me.

We'd lived in a small community cut off from the outside world.

My mother used to tell me about the earth before it burned. Our world was since called the Scorched Earth to always remember what once was.

No longer existing was separation by states and races. Each life form was free to choose where to live.

The creatures had returned and ventured a new beginning with humans, reappearing from the depth of the dreams and tales of humans.

My community had been afraid.

But Alrade the proof that it had worked, all lived together in harmony.

Two minutes had passed.

Is he going to drown himself?

I leaned over the counter, getting a better look at the pool.

No bubbles or other movements were to be seen.

I bit down on my lip.

I couldn't care less. *Why was I worried?*

Because he was a guest. Exactly, and only because of that.

He rose, a fountain hugging him. His hips close to the surface with his front facing me.

I plopped back on the chair, his piercing gaze seeking mine. His nose was straight, his chin strong, covered in a five o'clock shadow, his cheekbones reminded of a pointed knife.

Strands of his soaked dark hair clutched his skin, and I traced the pattern with my eyes.

He raised his arm, and I followed the movement.

Fingers with sharp claws curled and beckoned me to him.

I shook my head.

His eyebrow twitched.

His head tilted, as if tasting my battle.

Harsh lips forming the words, *come to me*, flashing a sharp canine biting down on a soft pink tongue.

I didn't want to, but he was a customer and I'm just a lowly employee; I warned myself.

No chance for me to get away.

But I wouldn't leave without a fight.

CHAPTER FOUR

THE DRAKON HAD DISAPPEARED.

Probably while I had been on my way through the changing rooms.

My pulse quickened, thudding in my throat.

That damn... no, I was glad he—

"Kaida, there's a client who demands your service." Rumlar barked at me from the side.

"Don't just stand here doing nothing. Therapy room two. Now!" He took off, satisfaction glazing his features.

I saw no end to my nerves as the day wore on. The resistance changed into the desire of escape.

Just a little longer.

I bared my teeth, resting my grip on the knob of the therapy room. Resentment crawled down my spine and settled at the base.

Let's see if this customer would pick himself war or peace.

I shoved the handle down.

The light was dim and grew in yellow streaks across the warm wood paneling. Music played from the speakers to muffle the sounds from the outside. Candles were lit to further bake the warmed room.

I remained rooted to the spot.

The potent smell of lemon and mountain dew hit my nose.

No way.

I released my grip around the handle and wiped my damp palms on my white cotton shorts. The lump in the pit of my stomach liquefied.

Calm down.

I had to be certain.

I looked at the recliner where my clients usually waited for me.

Indeed, there was someone already lying, and this someone was huge. I couldn't make out anything else except his tall figure, because a blanket covered the person.

Now, don't freak out. It's not him.

"Have you grown tight? Don't let the warm air escape!"

Damn.

It was his voice, wasn't it?

I could be mistaken. After all, he hadn't turned but mumbled his question into the pillow.

I shut the door.

Intending not to stay longer than needed.

I sneaked forward to the table, picked up the clipboard and skimmed the preferences and no-gos of the customer.

He demanded a vigorous massage, a full body massage to be exact.

Some of my clients mistook the massages, asking for special treatments.

I flipped the page. The client preferred an oil blended with cloves and wild yew.

Weird combo.

Stop.

Why do I care what his preferences are? I choose not to massage him if it's him.

I faced the client, freezing as I locked gazes with the pervert.

Him.

"Are you going to massage me already?" The Drakon laid there like a suitor. A fist under his cheek and bedroom eyes, which he lowered, acknowledging my change of clothes with pity written on his face.

My temper cut through my frozen body.

Shaking, I wished to spin around and flee.

I craved not to meet him.

But I braced myself. I would fight him and his arrogance. "Why did you leave?"

"Showing you your place."

I vibrated with the need to insult him.

To scream at him. Scratch him.

"That you do what I want." he continued.

I bit my lip. A metallic tang flooded my mouth. "You—" He cut me off. "Ah-ah-ah, you don't want to repeat what you had said earlier. Because I will make your life much worse."

This was a promise.

He knew Rumlar would not stand behind me, no matter what I told him.

He had me in the palm of his hand.

At his feet, if he wished.

I licked the trickle of blood from my mouth and sought to soothe my racing heart.

He followed my tongue and laughed. The vibrating of his vocal cords hit the sensitive spot of my center. My legs squeezed shut to get rid of any friction.

His dominance infested eyes liquefied my insides. The tenderness licking down my spine left me with nothing but a gooey mass in my mind.

"Thats what I thought." he nodded. "Now, do you want me to help you prepare the oil?"

"No!" Forcing a tad of sympathy into my voice. "I meant no, I can do it myself. Stay down."

I stretched my lips into a thin smile and gathered the ingredients for the oil.

I feared the suffocation that would run my system.

But I feared the aftereffects of staying longer in this room with him, more.

Feared that I would lace my hands around his powerful neck and press. Until he stopped making a sound.

I would cause him to suffer.

Placing two brass bowls and the natural ingredients in front of me, I poured the base oil in to one bowl.

"Please relax. I will mix the aromas. You should breathe deep while doing so for further enjoyment."

As long as you still can.

I added the clove blossoms, parts of the fruits and leaves of the wild yew into the other small bowl.

With a wooden mortar, I ground the two plants, and a marvelous fragrance lingered.

I would have had to wear gloves with these additives, but Rumlar had bought a base oil that was prepared by a witch to avoid possible poisoning.

Hence, our customers sought the direct contact with skin on skin. I could guess, but I didn't need to imagine why.

It was never difficult for me to give people what they preferred. I loved my work.

Relaxation, healing and human contact.

Everything was my responsibility. I decided how far I went and what I offered. Rumlar had never interfered. The only good thing about him. He was not a pimp, unlike other bathhouses.

Satisfied with the consistency the plants formed in the

brass bowl, I added the base oil into it and mixed the two parts together and was greeted by a lush green infused with golden streaks. *Like the eyes of the Drakon.*

I buried the dry retch with a cough that worked its way up.

Everything done. I had to enter the snake pit.

I placed the oil on the table next to the couch.

With trembling hands, I covered my palms with the disinfectant.

His hidden upper body moved in solid breathing.

"If you are ready, I'll start now?"

He grumbled.

"Very nice. If anything is wrong, let me know."

I flipped back the blanket covering his torso.

Marvelous.

I don't care! Silencing my stupid thoughts.

Not only on the front of his body were the crystalline scales spreading. They also spread across his back in patterns that made no sense. Likewise, the radiant veins stretched across it. With each pump of his heart, they flared in different places.

My breathing came in short waves I worked to steady and drizzled some oil onto his back.

Beads of oil trickled in quick trails along the sides of his back, eager to cover the front as well.

Goosebumps spread over the part of his human skin, the scales standing up.

Spreading some oil on my palms, I drew in a deep draught of the aroma, with my hands in front of my nose.

Ready.

Rubbing the oil on his human skin, I wasn't sure if I should even touch his scales.

He noticed my restraint.

"You can touch every part of my body. How else are you supposed to massage me?"

His voice rasped in my ears.

With the pressure of my fingers, I let him know I understood.

Now that I knew I could not hurt him or myself, I stroked the edge of the scales with my pinky.

They were soft and warm, unlike what I feared.

The warmth differed from that of a fire or a conventional heater. It jumped over to my limbs and warmed them from the inside.

A glistening warm light shifted before my inner eyes.

I sighed.

Fueled by the feeling in one finger, I mustered all my courage and let my hands wander upward, taking the sinewy muscles of his shoulders and easing them between my fingers.

"How do you even know I give massages?"

He chuckled.

"I saw your hands and figured this is the reason they are attached to your body."

"I can show you what these hands are capable of."

I squeezed, forcing his muscles to move in the direction I ordered.

He buzzed in delight.

I invoked my training and kneaded every muscle that was on his back. And there were quite a few. Whenever the lights under his skin touched my palms, I received a jolt. A jolt that shot straight to my stomach and flowed like liquid gold between my thighs.

I sank my hands deep into his back to feel for any tenderness and pressed down hard. His breathing had quickened, as if he had no sense I was struggling to make him stop the massage.

I moved on to the head of his shoulder, his muscular upper arm, and on down. As I progressed, the further I pulled his arm off the table to build tension and relaxation.

I rubbed over his hands, which were covered with calluses on the insides.

Next would be his fingers.

I dreaded those damn claws at the tips.

I nodded my head.

Slowly, I ran each limb of his index finger up and down in a circular motion. I took my time before I got all the way to the end, taking the clawed fingertip between my thumb and forefinger and rubbed. The muscles of his back tensed.

My heart galloped, imagining his claws on my skin. Rasping over delicate skin, threatening to open it wide when losing control.

I was losing control.

I ordered myself to keep my cool, speeding over each finger and finishing with his arm, taking his hand in mine, pulling and stretching it.

His claws scraped across my skin.

Jesus.

A thundershower of hot rain drops ignited by the spark frizzled through my system, leaving nothing but slick sweat in its path.

I had to end this.

Soon.

The outlook stopping in the middle of the session? Not to mention the consequences for my job.

I forced myself to continue and reached for his other arm, but spared any additional oil to urge him to finish this massage himself.

The unpleasantry didn't show as far as his breathing was getting ragged.

I feared my clothes might turn transparent again. Heavy

beads of sweat dripped from my hairline onto my forehead. The center of attention far below for my liking.

His skin warmed my hands but was without a bead of sweat. I couldn't be the only one who noticed.

Apparently, he could stand high temperatures.

I ended the massage on his arm and returned to his back.

Safe area. No more claws.

I sighed.

"Anything wrong?" he asked.

"No, everything is fine. Keep relaxing."

I kneaded downward from his mid-back to the next part of this massage, the base of his backsides, which continued to be hidden by the blanket.

Safe territory? This?

The spice of lemon and mountain dew came back in force and engulfed me whole. The storm inside me electrified and I could feel his breath speed up under my grip.

Imperceptibly, he rocked his hips against the recliner.

My fingers roamed over the base of his buttocks, my cheeks blushed, imagining him as he'd stood before me a few minutes ago.

Before I'd entered this room and rode into my personal hell.

Naked.

So absolutely blunt and arrogant.

I pushed the blanket further down and pinched his buttocks.

He drew in a sharp breath.

Nothing more than a gasp escaped from my lips.

Something brushed up against my leg.

Velvety soft over the inside of my thigh.

My chest constricted, and my nipples pebbled.

He only drove his hips harder into the couch.

A growl escaped him.

I snapped. "What are you doing?"

I jumped from his vibrating body.

His tail hung out from under the blanket.

If he hadn't touched me with his hands, then he'd just had used—

"Pervert! What were you doing?" I should have left.

"Giving you what your body has been begging me for all this time."

"Fucking bullshit." I thundered.

The moment the curse fell from my mouth, I gasped. I opened and folded my hands by my side, trying to stuff my temper back into its cage.

It was too late.

"How dare you treat me like a piece of shit? How dare you humiliate me by coming to you and then vanish? How dare you touch me without my permission, assuming I was the one wanting this?" I raised my arms and gestured around me. "And listen. If you never heard of it: That's just my fucking stupid body reacting to your physical touch for no common reason other than biology."

He kept laying there, indifferently. No sign if he listened or not.

"So get that message to your brain and stop assuming things. Better, change your view on the world, especially around women."

Fucking shit.

I should have refused right away. "I'm done with this. I'm leaving. Don't you dare inform my boss and I expect to be paid in full!" I headed for the door.

A breeze swirled strands into my face.

He stood in front of me, strong fingers lacing around my arm.

I tried to push him away.

He stepped back. Surprised by the force I'd put into the push, he stumbled.

Dragging me with him, his fingers pushing down hard into my flesh. His claws leaving additional marks.

We crashed and with it went the guttural rage I had felt, sliding down the serpentines of my brain.

He groaned in pain underneath me.

That didn't just happen.

I'd hurt a customer.

My gaze wandered to his eyes.

I didn't see the anger and arrogance I'd expected.

The inside of his green dragon eye spun in slow circles of white and yellow. Not just green, not just juniper or olive, but a blend of every pigment: sun rays and darkness, dregs of nature, thirst and insidious arousal.

His breath came hitching from his moist lips.

Sparks rolled through my hips and chest where our skin kissed, gasping for air.

I tore my gaze and leaned from my elbows onto my hands, ripping my breasts free.

I'd meant what I'd said, that I found him arrogant and sick. But I would lie calling him hideous.

I don't know if I'd told him or kept it a secret.

Either way, he wasn't hideous, not in a physical way.

He was probably the most handsome man that I would ever get close in my life. His tall, mighty body was perfect, cocooning my petite body in comparison. Features symmetrical, masculine and illusory. His claws knew how to reap pleasure.

His cock pressing against my stomach was the dream material of every desperate housewife.

Yet his character was rotten and because of that, I found him utterly unattractive.

The silent gunfight between us lasted for far too long, making my arms tremble. I wouldn't let him see it.

I was far too aware of what he could do to me, since I had too long to cool down.

He could crush me.

He could crush everything I had and worked for. Not just my job, but my soul.

I pushed myself up.

My sudden reaction drawn me as the prey he so desperately wanted.

In one second, he grabbed my wrists and pulled them over his head, pressing me into submission, with me on top of him.

His powerful throat corded with muscle, and a vein pumped as he let loose.

I arched up, trying to remove his hold.

My chest pressed down, down, down on his and forcing my breath in hiccups.

He shuddered.

The heat of his body radiated into mine. From my cheeks to my breasts to my core.

He freed one of his hands, closing around my wrist with only one. I wiggled, trying to use the change of control with no use.

He scratched over my side, caressing my contours with his claws, touching the globes of my breasts flattened against his chest.

I pressed my legs together. A low moan escaped him.

Caught in his gaze, I was smothered by the scent of fresh mountain spring and lemon.

His hard on grew beneath me.

My nipples rubbed over his scale speckled chest.

Shackled around my ankle was his tail, again.

Creeping up, up, up, touching the rim of my butt and under my shorts.

"Say it. Say you want this as much." He rasped, his hips pressing in need of friction against me.

Startled, I pulled the air between my lips, my eyes widening in magnitude. Reminding myself of the situation at hand.

I wrenched out of his grip, both from his arms and his gaze.

He hissed and tried to jump up as well.

It was at that moment I noticed his nakedness and a gleaming from his lap.

I sprawled my hands before my eyes, not wanting to see anything.

He laid flat when I stumbled around him and out the door.

CHAPTER FIVE

I WAS LIVID.

Not only had I been knocked to the ground, forced to take the plunge myself, and finally gotten rid of Sid. Only to end up with the most hideous person, creature or whatever, who could've ever crossed my path.

Crushing my locker shut after I'd changed, my phone buzzed in my pocket.

The local police station.

I sighed.

Not today.

What could they possibly want?

But reason prevailed.

"Hi this is Kaida Whyte." My vocal cords tingled with anger.

"Miss Whyte, I'm the prosecutor for your case, Levana Blackbourne. Please call me Levana. Glad that I could reach you. I'd tried several times."

"I'd been working."

And could finally go, I added in my head.

"Great. Could you please come over? I have some questions left before the hearing."

"Sure. I'm leaving just now. I'll be there in 20 minutes."

I walked by foot to clear out my thoughts, not wanting to let Levana suffer at the police station from my urge to kill someone.

All thanks to that prick.

He had not dared to balk me again. Which was best for him.

It was already dark. Insects flew to the light of the street lamps. A gentle summer breeze blew through my hair and kissed my sweaty neck.

I wasn't sure what they needed me for.

I hugged my chest tighter and pressed my jacket, which I had slung over my arm, against me. Forcing the memories of Sid to stay inside me.

The police department was already in sight. Only a few people were on the streets tonight. They probably were at the park or the sea to celebrate the beginning of summer.

"Excuse me?"

I turned around and took a step back.

A man with a hood pulled deep over his face stood in a nook.

Backtracking, I gazed for the police station.

A jolt caught me, and I crashed, my teeth clinking together.

The man on top of me.

I had no time to think about the impact. Hands wrapped around my neck and squeezed.

I fought.

Cold sweat coated my skin.

My legs kicking for him.

I scratched his hands, tried to reach his face to inflict any pain on him, for me to move out of his grip.

I had no chance.

Tears streamed down my cheeks.

My chest tightened painfully.

I let my head fall to the side and looked in the direction of the police station. There was no one to help me.

Past horrors stirred up in my heart.

I knew what would wait at the end of this.

A glistening light broke from above the man, making me blind.

Utter warmth radiated from the source.

Not true.

This is how the final process of dying had to feel...

The pressure lifted off of me.

My lungs begged me to take a breath.

I tried to concentrate on the warmth, that would take me from this place of coldness.

A scream echoed, and I sucked in the cold night air.

I could not grasp what was happening in front of me.

A dragon stood on the street and bared its bloody teeth.

I couldn't make out where he started or ended. He was massive.

I thought they were extinct.

He stood before me with a frightening awareness, not only illuminated by the streetlight, his own light radiated strongly.

Why I knew he was male?

I didn't.

It just called deep inside me.

Enormous viridian eyes sat tightly within the bony skull, which gave the creature a fierce-looking appearance.

Several small crystal growths sat atop his head, just above his large, curved ears.

Fan-like skin and bone structures ran down the sides of each of his jaw lines.

His nose was stubby and had two long, pointy nostrils, and there was a small tendril on its chin. Several sharp teeth covered in blood poked out from the side of his mouth and previewed the terror hiding inside.

A wide neck ran down from his head and into a bulky body. The top was covered in crystal-like skin and a row of small tendrils ran down its spine.

The bottom covered in radiant skin and colored slightly lighter than the rest of his body.

The prettiest color of turquoise and purple soothed my pounding heart.

Four bulky limbs carried his body and allowed the creature to stand elevated and proud. Each limb had six digits, each of which ended in pointy nails seemingly made of crystal.

Delicate wings grew, starting from just below his shoulders, and ended all the way down at his pelvis. The wings were almost butterfly-like, the edges of the skin inside the wings tattered and damaged and jagged edges at the bottom almost gave it a feathered look.

His simple tail ended in a single tendril and was covered in the same crystal-like skin as the body.

He looked at me almost angrily, and the light that flowed through his body intensified.

Shouting nudged my ears and police officers stormed from the station. Some gathered around the man that attacked me, other came running to my side.

"Miss, are you alright? Please stay down. The ambulance will be here shortly."

I tried to look past them, since no one seemed to notice the dragon that had rescued me.

I peered around, but he was gone and neither of the officers spoke to me about it.

∾

I'd sat on the bed in the ambulance that was parked in front of the police station, waiting.

The doctor had given me clearance, he'd told me I was fine, just some bruises around my neck.

I reclined the offer for psychological help, reassuring him I knew what would come these next days.

I needed no one to talk to. I needed this fucking shit to be over and done.

"Miss Whyte?"

I knew that voice only now it was full of compassion and uncertainty.

Tearing my gaze up, the Drakon stood in front of me.

"What are you doing here?" I said.

He raised an eyebrow.

"I work here."

No way. That was the least I could use right now.

Besides his pity.

I pushed past him and turned. "Lead the way." I said.

He grumbled and lead me in. Inside, he opened the door where the prosecutor, Miss Blackbourne, waited for me.

Blood red painting her lips.

Revealing her fangs and nature with a smile.

A vampire.

She greeted me and monitored me to take a seat on the only chair that sat in front of a small table, opposite her's.

This room held no comfort.

"Thanks for your attendance and I'm so sorry about what had happened."

"Thank you. Do you know what the man had wanted and where that dragon came from?"

"Kaida, I might call you by your first name?"

I shrugged.

"Great. Are you alright?" she asked.

32

"I'm fine. Could you make your point? I want to go home."

"Of course. He was one of the people we were looking for. One that you had named us, that cooperated with your ex-boyfriend. And he'd wanted to kill you."

A tide of ice doused down my spine.

"Thats why you wanted to see me today?" I asked.

"We-w..." She hesitated, looking at the Drakon.

"Just say it." I barked.

"We knew that this man was following you for a while now. We also knew that he'd wanted to strike today." She spoke without taking a breath. "Thats why we'd asked you to come in today so we could get him. We had patrols the whole way. The dragon you saw is working with us."

"You work with dragons?" I asked. The only thing that sprang to my mind.

"Indeed—"

"Stop." I halted. The amount of what they had done dribbled in.

I shot up; the chair falling.

"To make sure I heard that right. You knew what would happen and didn't think to tell me? What are those games you play at the police?" I asked and bared my teeth.

"Kaida, please, we couldn't tell you. He was listening to all your phone calls. This decision was well thought."

I marched to the door.

The Drakon stood in my way, grabbing my elbow.

I glared at his hand. "Let me go. And you..." I said, turning my head to Levana. "A heads up was the least you could have done."

"I'm sorry—" she said.

I struggled in his hold.

"Let me the fuck go." I said and pushed against his stone body.

"Jaro, please let her go." Levana said. "But Kaida, you need to stay here a little longer. Everyone knows. No way to sneak out."

I pushed him aside and was out the door and went to the women's restroom.

Shutting the door, I slammed my fists into the tiles.

Not only had they betrayed me, but they had grounded me.

I couldn't stop fisting the tiles. Blood spreading with each hit.

I yelled until my hands could no more.

Memories of Sid and the many nights that were not blissful came back and tried to overwhelm me.

I let them.

Opening my arms for the pain to swallow me whole.

I was nothing anymore except my memories.

I don't know how much time had faded, but someone knocked at the door.

"Come in." I said. My voice broken from the screaming.

It was the Drakon.

Jaro.

Heat shot into my cheeks.

"Please come with me. Everything is ready for you to leave." His eyes smeared with hesitation.

"You seem uncertain about it." I said.

"There is one more thing."

I didn't care. Whatever they wanted.

I just wanted to get out of here and into my bed, no more strength left to fight. "Fine. Lead the way."

Levana leaned at the receptions desk waiting for us. I held my gaze down, not ready to meet any of their faces.

"Kaida, can you stay with someone today?" she asked.

"No. I have a home of my own."

"We thought so. The court and me placed you under

protection. Officer Bishop will take you home with him and have an eye on you till the court hearing."

I blinked my eyes, fathoming what I just heard.

I faced Jaro, who stood behind me.

"Do you think this is a fucking joke?" I said.

"No, indeed it's not. I have a room that was just left by my former roommate and this is my job. Miss Whyte." He said, lengthening the end of my name.

Bloody bastard!

Levana hit the desk with her hand, breaking through the silence of everyone listening around us.

My body twitched, and I sought the vampire's gaze.

"Great. Since we settled everything, you are free to go home with Officer Bishop."

"WHY DIDN'T YOU SAY ANYTHING TO ME AT THE SPA? YOU LET me massage you, enjoyed humiliating me, and then you almost let someone strangle me to death. Where was your fucking help? What kind of fucked up person are you?"

I tore apart the silence inside his car.

"I—" he said.

"Don't. Just don't. I want to plug my ears with a knife if I have to hear anymore words from your mouth."

I glanced sideways. Stubbornness glazed his features.

The lights from outside speed over his perfect form I wanted to punch so desperately.

He remained silent while we turned in a street that was full of big houses, probably to house big creatures like him.

He stopped in front of one. The front door was probably eight feet high and baby blue against the brick wall. On top was a flat roof with a railing.

He nodded to the door, leaving the car without a word, and I followed.

His back tensed, pushing past the seams of his white shirt. The jacket that goes with his uniform hung loose around his arm. His ass squeezed in black slacks. He looked more like a CEO than an officer. His attitude would rather be fitting.

He unlocked the door and stepped aside, his hand showing me in.

I had no choice. I knew a lot more of Sid's people were out there. The guy that had attacked me was merely a semi-big fish. There were several to go and until I made my testimony, I couldn't risk to get caught. I could worry what my life would be after I got the money and Sid was behind bars.

The door slammed shut.

The hallway was wide and built with high walls, and yet he cramped me, with his powerful body and the closed door in my back.

His presence lurking at the corners of my brain. Unsure what to do with him or were to put his actions. He sure hadn't taken me in because he was a savior, or to fuck me at least. The question remained: what were his motives?

Pent up air escaped his lungs, and he pushed past me, further down the hall to one of the many doors leading off of it.

He opened a door and faced me.

"Here's your room. It's not much, but it should be enough for the time being."

I stormed past him, giving him the finger, and shut the door in his face.

"You're welcome." His voice was muffled behind the door. Another door opened and shut.

The room was decorated in bordeaux. In the center was

a large bed, which was enveloped by a fine fabric from above.

I wrapped my arms around my chest and dropped face first onto the bed. Tenderly, the soft material stroked my cheek.

A scent of grapes and roses soothed me to sleep. Forgotten the wounds that needed attendance on my hands.

CHAPTER SIX

My senses stirred, and the weight of last night hit me in the guts.

I'd woken several times and contemplated the lack of my fight.

I looked totally unable to care for myself, pressing my palms into my eyes.

I'm so miserable.

What does he want from me?

What was he gaining from this? I couldn't believe that he did it because the court ordered him too. He must have said that he had a spare room. They wouldn't force him to take me in, would they?

With a tortured groan, I worked my naked body out of the blankets.

My brain threatened to burst already early in the morning.

I needed to clean my system of them.

I entered the connected bathroom I found last night and went under the spray of hot water, washing away the traces of last night.

Dried blood liquified and flowed down the drain. I'd

completely forgotten to take care of my hands. Right now, the wounds had formed a crust that kept them from bleeding.

Flexing my fingers showed no major pain. But I should portably still check in with a doctor to see if I had broken something.

Maybe I would ask Jaro to take me to a doctor.

I stepped out after I'd almost burned my skin and awaken my senses, putting on the clothes from yesterday.

Following the aroma of coffee through the hall, I entered the oversized kitchen.

The much bigger something in it that room, blushing my cheeks, was Jaro.

He sat bent over a newspaper and sipped his coffee in peace.

I had hoped to get a coffee first.

"How long are you going to stand there rooted to the spot?" he asked.

A fake laugh left my lips, and I shuffled further into the room.

"Good morning Jaro." I said, waiting for a reaction that told me I wasn't allowed to use his name, but it failed to materialize.

"Good morning Kaida. It seems you slept well judging from your change in attitude."

My attitude was his concern?

"Vice versa."

I slammed into the chair across from him.

"There she is. Would you like coffee?"

He stood up.

"Yes. Let's stop this small talk, then. What do you want from me?" I asked.

He poured the coffee and handed me the cup with a phony smile, falling back into his chair.

His eyes settled on my face and I could almost see the answer he wanted to give me, but refused to.

"Nothing. Just doing my job and babysitting you. Doesn't that sound fun?"

His lips curled at the word fun.

"Yeah, real fuuun."

"You know what? If it wasn't my job, I wouldn't be bothered."

I leaned forward. "Then let me leave."

"No, you will stay down here with me and enjoy my company as I like to give it to you." he said.

"Ha, I think you are out of your mind—"

"Now is not your time to talk. It's mine. You will be respectful to me in my home. And about your questions from last night."

He put the word questions in quotation marks with his fingers. "I couldn't have said anything because I didn't know you were Kaida Whyte."

He clenched his jaw.

"And for the strangling, I had no part in that. As you should have learned by now, I'm just an officer." He bit down on each word, growing louder.

I dropped my gaze.

How could I trust him and the answers he gave me?

I slid my gaze over to his clawed hands. Down to his legs that disappeared under the table and I wondered how much more of his skin was occupied by the shimmering scales.

Under my gaze, he darted in his chair.

He didn't seem to enjoy being looked at like that.

A light scent of citrus and mountain dew emanated from him, intensifying with each stroke of my eyes.

The glow under his skin pulsated more.

"What is it about the light under your skin?" I asked.

He exhaled heavily, but did not immediately follow up with an answer.

My gaze continued to wander down to his tail, which came up next to him in light thuds on the ground.

The very same tail that had touched me twice. I now inspected him. Strong towards the base, which I could not see. It ran further and further down and narrowed to the end. After the narrowest part was overcome, a part as a rhombus followed.

"How can you sit on your—uh—I mean tail?" I asked.

He choked on his coffee and coughed violently.

His face turned red, which I blamed on the coughing fit.

I rose and patted him on the back.

Each pat gave me one of those shocks.

He turned away from me, away from my hands that touched him, like acid that threatened to scald him.

After he calmed down, he stood up and pushed past me without touching me.

"I'm sorry but... since they had ordered me to work inside today, I have some paperwork to take care of." *That was prompt.* "Do I have your respect?"

"Ok and when can—what can I do?" Ignoring his question.

He swirled around and pressed me against the wall.

His hip connecting with my body.

The beautiful face of his was just mere millimeters away. His eyes latched onto my lips. I draught in small breaths, not wanting to repeat his reaction from yesterday.

Black shards of lust filled his eyes. He leaned closer, and I closed my eyes.

But instead of my mouth, soft flesh met my neck, leaving a wet trace behind.

"Do I have your respect?"

He reinforced his question with the pressure of his hips.

More like a command for obedience.

"Yes. Now leave!"

I thrust my hands against his chest.

Another trace of salvia and sharp fangs was his answer. Showing me who was in control.

"You better get back to bed. I'm going to be unresponsive for a few hours."

His words and touch just a whisper with his sudden leave.

I HAD LAIN DOWN AS PER HIS REQUEST, BUT I WAS OVER IT soon.

Over doing nothing and over his attitude towards me.

He could go to hell and I would not wait and lie here when he summons me.

This overbearing asshole.

He meant he had me in his hands, but I was just biding my time in his home, showing somewhat of respect. But my time to make him pay would come.

I got up and looked out of my room into the hallway. All doors were closed except one.

A calm wind seemed to blow from it, carrying the scent of the morning inside.

Sunlight, that would be just the thing for me now.

I moved out of my room and opened the door further and indeed, on a few steps, followed another door through which light bathed the staircase in warmth.

A tingling sensation spread inside me.

I climbed the stairs and through the second door greeted me a beautiful roof terrace.

Such a gem up here.

The view stretched infinitely far, to the mountain peaks that surrounded our city, forcing peace in me.

I wasn't sure if I was still angry, pissed, or just tired from everything. Again, he had been the asshole he was, and he didn't want to have me, but still he had me.

Observing him showed me he was not the arrogant CEO that wouldn't butch. He reacted to me.

Would it be any good to water his insults down?

I needed to stay here a little longer. Why should I put a hardship on myself and he was decent at the being this morning?

I sighed, unsure of what to do.

A cough broke through my thoughts, and I turned.

It was Jaro, standing in front of me with a bottle of wine and two glasses in his hands.

"Peace offering?" he asked.

I raised my eyebrow in a frown. "It's just about noon."

He shrugged and walked to the garden swing seat at the other end of the rooftop terrace.

"Hey, I don't make the rules around here, besides I'm done working. The paperwork didn't take me as long as I thought it would after all."

I laughed.

"First, am I really worthy of your presence and second, why the peace offering?"

"Come over here and sit down first." He said, tapping next to him.

I took a deep breath and braced myself.

He had already filled both glasses to the brim. I took the glass and sat down next to him.

He straightened his legs and I did the same. He dug his feet into the ground and set the swing in motion. A bubbly laugh escaped me.

What a childlike mannerism.

For a while we sat sipping our wine, enjoying the sun tanning our skin and the view of the mountains climbing high into the sky.

"You know..." he began, "I love the mountains."

I laughed and turned to him.

"What?" he asked.

"Nothing. I'm just wondering where that came from." I barely brought out my stomach cramping. "What are you, a thousand years old?" His grin died on his face. "No. Are you kidding me?"

But instead of answering, he just looked grimly into his glass and emptied it in one go.

"Sorry, I didn't mean to tease you."

I liked that he was the one squirming right now. Finally, a time were he was submitting.

"Never mind." he said.

With this answer, he only aroused more interest in me.

Even though I thought it was cute that he was just acting like a little boy. Of all the things I thought of him, that was the reaction I would have least suspected.

"Really, I'm sorry." I held out my hand. "Let's start from the beginning. I'm Kaida Whyte, the patronizing one for today. Nice to meet you and thank you for letting me stay with you."

With a grin, he took my hand in his, and immediately small sparks jumped from him to me.

His face darkened when he looked at my hand.

I wanted to pull it away, but he took my other hand from my lap and covered both with his hands.

A light escaped the cracks between our fingers, and warmth radiated into my hands.

He lifted one hand and the wounds on my hands were gone.

What the heck!

"What do you offer?" His lace covered voice dropped a few octaves.

"I beg you pardon?"

He leaned forward, gripping my hands tight.

"I meant it. What do you offer?" he asked.

I snatched my hand from him and threw a fist. That he caught just in front of his face and laughed uproariously.

"You ass, what are you doing?"

"It's called revenge." An evil grin wrapped around his lips.

I stood from the swing and walked over to the edge of the roof terrace and leaned over it. Taking in the freedom the wind offered so willingly.

I sensed Jaro behind me and turned to face him. He was looking up at the sky, his head lifted, the wind blowing through his loose hair.

I turned completely around and lifted myself onto the edge of the terrace. I stumbled and Jaro got hold of my arms.

"Careful, or do you want to fall to your death?"

"No."

He took a few steps back.

"Revenge for what?" I asked.

"For you laughing at me because of my love for the mountains. Now we are back to even."

"Is your life only a game?" I asked.

"Who knows? But to answer your initial question. We're in this situation together, and I think we both could need a breather. I wanted to apologize for my behavior yesterday."

"The one in the bathhouse?"

"No." Played horrified, he looked at me.

"For being so brusque with you last night."

"Ah... okay."

That was the part he regretted the most, not his attitude at the bathhouse.

I was glad that we were on the same page for my forced stay at his home.

"So, do you accept my apology?" he asked, moving closer again.

We would be together for only a few more hours. Why not pretend I was okay with his apology and imagine he had actual motives behind the way he acted?

"Yeah sure. Ehm. It was a pretty weird situation and I could still bite myself in the ass for not rejecting it. So not that I don't appreciate it here now." Pointing between us.

He gave me a genuine smile.

My breath caught in my throat.

His beautiful smiling face was close to mine, for the second time this day.

For an eternity, we looked at each other in silence and Jaro drifted towards me, his eyes fixated on my lips.

I recoiled and staggered.

I toppled backwards over the edge and closed my eyes, praying it would go quickly.

And I screamed.

CHAPTER SEVEN

I WOULD DIE. HIT THE GROUND LIKE A RIPE MELON AND BURST.

The free fall wreaked havoc in my body and mind.

The wind tore at my clothes. Seconds became hours, and hours became days.

I had hoped that I would fall unconscious mid flight but—

A jolt went through my whole body.

I opened my eyes only a crack.

Jaro's face was close to mine, wiping away every thought that had arisen.

The feeling of falling ebbed away.

"Will you take me to the other side?"

A deep rumble gripped my body.

Something like guilt reflected in his gaze as he scanned my body.

My neck and legs tingled where he wrapped his arms around tight.

I was utterly confused.

His searching gaze sought my eyes, and he laughed.

"Why are you laughing?" I asked.

He stopped, and I was already missing the feeling of what it triggered in me.

"Just your deliciously confused look that tells me everything I need to know. Like before."

My face flushed red, which earned me another laugh.

He cleared his throat. "Are you afraid of heights? If so, close your eyes because it is already too late."

We stretched through the air, my eyes on him and words failing me.

Like literally flying.

I screamed again.

We were definitely going to die.

I pressed my face against his chest and there it was, the scent that had been haunting me. It was indeed his scent and right now it was intensifying, soothing me, just as his arms around my body strengthened.

"Don't be afraid lit—" he stopped himself.

I dared to look at him again, and this time I looked past him.

Wings stretched out behind his back that had cushioned my fall to death.

Beautiful gossamer wings.

"How?" Was all I could think about in this moment.

"Later" he said. "You should better relish the view."

And I did.

With me in his arms, we shot above the terrace of his house towards the mountains and over the several houses of the city.

It was magnificent, and I eased into his embrace.

"Why do you love the mountains? Please, I won't laugh again."

I could see him contemplating, but whatever it took him to decide, he did.

"I love the mountains and not because I'm old, but

because I'd loved being there when my parents were bugging me as usual."

He tried to make it sound lighthearted, but in his eyes I saw a glimmer of sadness and also maybe anger.

"Sounds nice. But how old are you really?" I couldn't hold back my curiosity.

"You needy little thing. I knew there is a great hunger in you." He said, not able to move out of his skin an inch. "Well, I don't know what you know about my kind?"

He looked at me, waiting.

What should I answer him?

That I had absolutely no idea, although I'd lived here like forever...

"Not very much."

"Ok, then this will all sound pretty absurd to you. I'm actually 70 years old."

I swallowed.

"But in human years, I'm only 35 years old. We age more slowly, and so we don't grow until later."

„How long do you live?"

"Most of us live to be 600 years old and die at exactly the same age as humans. But there are also stories that point to a much longer lifespan. But I don't know anyone personally."

"I see." My gaze tilted downward.

"No need to be sad. We can have our fun long enough and when you finally die, I would just look for another bride."

Who would have thought he had a funny side to share?

"Should you really be flying? Drunk? Besides, what would I want with someone like you? Who constantly wants to kiss me without being asked?"

He just grinned broadly.

"It must really be the wine or the sun that has been hard

on you. Or maybe your brain hasn't developed properly along with it?"

"Careful. You seem to think my brain hadn't developed, but I'd developed just the right things, I can assure you."

He landed us light as a feather back on his rooftop and held me for a moment longer.

A tender feeling of a flame blazed in my heart and sprayed from there through my whole body.

I squirmed under his gaze and the reaction building inside me, jumping from his arms. Distancing myself.

His wings disappeared behind his back.

"How?" I circled him to find his shirt in tatters on his back.

"I'm not just a Drakon, but a Shifter. I can summon parts to add to my body. This includes my wings..."

"What is the difference between what you can use and what you can't? What is permanent in your current form?"

"Everything you see right now is permanent."

I slid my eyes again over his body. Over the parts that were covered in clothing. And didn't know what lurked underneath them.

"I could very well show you what is under this close if you keep continue to undress me with your eyes. And stop looking at my tail. This is a private matter." His Tail twitching in response on the floor.

I gasped and waved my hands. "I didn't do that. You must have been—"

Interrupted by the growling in my stomach, he laughed at me.

"I see you might as well be hungry, but for proper food."

Before I could say anything, he went to the door leading into the house.

"I'll buy some food. Don't make yourself fall again while I'm away. Don't open the door to anyone and you're welcome." He said over his shoulder and vanished into the house.

He'd left. His insults running through my blood. Hot and needy.

Something I hadn't felt in months and only since I'd first met him.

If not in years.

If not at all.

CHAPTER EIGHT

I LINGERED ON HIS TERRACE UNTIL THE SUN HAD SETTLED.

By the time I went downstairs, Jaro was already gone.

My body was still tingling and infected by his gentle side. I couldn't sit still.

A trip around his apartment couldn't hurt.

If the rooms I had seen were already well designed, the rest of his house could only be better.

What his bedroom would look like?

I had to know.

This fantasy had to be resolved for me.

His front door in my back. I thrust my hands on my hips.

Only three doors remained I hadn't seen.

I opened the first of the doors to my left.

The stars and the moon poured in through the vast windows.

Almost like standing outside.

I flicked on the light. Inside was a gigantic living room. The biggest part of the room was the sofa. Pillows piling up on it. Behind a dining table that could seat a good six people. Opposite the sofa was a sideboard on which stood a large TV.

I moved into the room and approached the sideboard.

No dust, everything was spotless. However, there were also no pictures that could have offered any insights.

Not even books.

It wasn't a living room, but an exhibition room.

I opened the next door after leaving the room.

This room was dark and tinged in its fragrance.

Either this room had no windows or they were covered.

I felt over the wall next to me for the light switch when I touched something soft.

I jumped back and jerked my hand in front of my face.

There was nothing on it.

Calm down, try again. What could it be?

I reassured myself and reached for the soft something again.

The light switch had to be in that exact spot.

I pressed down and the light came on.

Amazement painted my features.

The darkness of the walls almost swallowed the light. Heavy curtains blocked every source of it.

The switch was covered in fur.

Artificial fur, I hoped.

An easel sat in front of the windows. With a painting that seemed unfinished.

I stepped closer without inspecting the rest of the room further, fascinated by it.

Everything shrouded in black.

But amid the blackness that seemed to swallow everything like a black hole, something blue shone.

A pair of blue piercing eyes from a woman.

It shook me and I rubbed my upper arms. A deep sadness clawed at me.

I didn't wanted to look at the painting anymore and looked around.

53

He seemed to sleep in here. A rumpled blanket and pillows were thrown on the sofa in this room. That would also explain the intense smell.

The room scared me and I couldn't stand it any longer.

It was as if I had to look into the depths of my soul.

I left.

His bedroom should be behind the last door.

Anticipation bubbled in my belly.

Carefully, I opened it and stuck my head inside.

Stroked by his scent.

I stepped inside without turning on the light. Enough, the light that shone through the windows.

Without my doing, I moved to his bed and stroked with my index finger over the sheets.

Damn soft.

I wanted to bury my nose in it.

No, Kaida. You can't do that, you freak.

The temptation to absorb his scent was too great. I bent down and pressed my nose into the fabric.

Delicious.

A shiver ran down my spine.

I could almost feel his hands on my back, sliding up and down.

A whimper escaped me and I was sure he would know that I wanted to feel his claws on me.

He would give in and start in the crook of my neck.

And oh my god, that feeling.

This mix of pleasure and fear of his claws would overwhelm me.

Something fell to the floor next to me with a crash.

I was discovered, wheeling around.

But no one was to be seen.

I stumbled to the door and pressed the switch.

A book on the floor. I must have knocked it off his nightstand.

I picked it up and put it back in its place.

Hopefully, he wouldn't notice.

I returned to my room before I could get caught.

I dropped onto my bed and leaned my head against the headboard.

For a moment, I held my breath and listened for more sounds.

Nothing.

I was ready to give into that feeling he evoked in me. That no one had ever done.

I assured myself that this would be a step to claim myself again.

Do it once and be over with the reaction his body held over mine.

I let my hand wander under my shorts and into my pants.

Already wet. I hissed.

I closed my eyes and stroked my breasts with my other hand.

Slowly, I moved my fingers up and down my most sensitive spot.

I gasped for air, the heat inside me immeasurably high.

The heat in my body burned down on my clothe and I got rid of my bra and shorts.

Wearing only my panties, I laid back down between the sheets.

I let my thoughts wander to when I massaged him.

Even now I could remember the roundness under the blanket that was his backside. Not to forget when I'd seen him in flesh.

I shivered and intensified my touch.

My nipples ached for his touch.

I dipped my index finger inside me, making me twitch. I longed for his lips to kiss every inch of my heated flesh and take my nipples into his mouth one by one, teasing them.

I was feverish.

My mind went to his claws on me. They were on the insides of my thighs and moved in slow circles further to my middle.

I pushed another finger in and massaged with the other hand my clit.

I was sure he could fill me.

And with that a storm seethed inside me and I climaxed, flashes before my eyes.

My gasps turned into unrestrained moans that echoed through my room, and I rode my climax as long as I could.

Bent over me, Jaro continued to cheer me on.

Startled, I wrenched my eyes open.

There was no one but me, sweaty and satisfied between his sheets.

Thank God.

That was quick. I giggled.

I hoped this would do the trick for my stupid body and his reactions towards Jaro.

There was nothing to be ashamed of. I had reclaimed something very important in my life. Besides, I had just escaped death again, and he was nice to me. So there was nothing bad about it.

My throat demanded an enormous glass of water, so I threw on my shirt and headed for the kitchen.

I entered the room, and at the table sat Jaro.

"Back so soon?" I squeaked, my voice betraying me.

I hoped he hadn't heard me. Not sure how much I had let myself go for anyone to hear.

He sniffed the air.

He stiffened, musing at me from narrow eyes from top to

bottom. His gaze lingered longer on my breasts, which had to show under my shirt.

He jerked, and his chair fell, crashing to the floor.

Wordlessly, he raced past me and slammed the door to his bedroom shut.

Only a deep rumble echoed, and the sound of something breaking.

Shit.

CHAPTER NINE

I HAD BARRICADED MYSELF IN MY ROOM FOR TWO HOURS AND had ran a path into the plush carpet.

Again and again, I'd stopped at the door, checking whether I could hear him.

But nothing.

I still prayed he had heard nothing.

Maybe I could explain to him I had bumped into something.

I held my stomach when he growled again.

It was already evening, and I hadn't eaten anything yet.

I couldn't take it any longer and decided to look for Jaro to tell him my big, fat lie.

Sticking my head into the hallway, I could hear his voice softly from the living room. Apparently, he left his room.

One more thing that spoke of a quality home. One couldn't hear what happened in the room next to you.

That means he may had not heard my moans.

I pushed all the way to the living room door.

Through the crack, I could see him.

He was talking on the phone and ruffling his hair.

"Listen, I can keep her here with me until the hearing,

but after that we have to find a solution quickly and tell her about the threats."

Threats?

I thought that was over.

He was silent for a moment.

"It's okay, I'll take care of it. I have to go."

I lifted my gaze, and he was now facing me.

Everything inside me was spinning, and I had to dry retch.

"Kaida, you shouldn't have heard that."

He came up to me and took my upper arms.

His touch tried to stop the chills that raged unnoticed inside me.

"Come, sit here." He led me to the sofa and pushed me down.

"Why? I thought it was over."

"I'm sorry. I won't lie to you, but the police received more threats, should you testify."

My body was shaking violently and tears etched down my face, leaving ugly marks.

This could not be. I had done everything and told everything.

Why couldn't anyone do anything about it? Why should my suffering not end at this point?

"Shh, calm down Kaida, I'm here."

He stroked my back, which I only noticed from a distance.

I let myself fall forward and clutched my knees.

"No, no, no. This just can't be happening. What else do I have to suffer? I can't take any more, Jaro."

He stayed beside me and let me be.

"I'd survived and had mustered up the courage to turn him in and confess everything to the police. What had I suffered these damn two years for? I don't want this anymore."

"I can't imagine what that must have been like for you, but I'm here and the hearing is going to finish him and everyone else that's in there. For months, I'd been working on nothing else."

I looked up at him.

"You're working on my case?"

"Yes. That's why I'd been assigned to take care of you. But I'd only known your name and hadn't seen a picture. I promise I hadn't known you worked in the Bathhouse."

My stomach growled again, and as bizarre as the situation was, I laughed.

I was run over by the bus, but my hunger didn't seem to mind.

"Come with me," he said and took my hand. "I've been cooking and was actually just coming to get you." Forgotten what had happened earlier.

I was glad for any distraction he wanted to give me and went with him to the kitchen.

There were already two plates of pasta on the table.

"That smells heavenly." With that, I earned myself a smile.

"Enjoy it."

I dug in and he did the same.

We ate in silence for a while and I saw Jaro wanted to say something but held back—

"If it helps, you are more then welcome to tell me about it. Maybe it will help ease your mind a little."

I wondered if it was smart to tell him about it, but I felt so comfortable in his presence and he had already told me something about himself before.

"Besides, I can handle more than most people." he added.

With a nod, I affirmed myself.

"I had met Sid at a friend's party and at first he'd been nice. We were together for three years and after half a year, he'd asked me if I wanted to move in with him. I'd agreed, since I hadn't been making that much on my salary as a massage therapist. Later, he'd lost his job at the garage and sank into alcohol. When he'd started inviting dubious people to our apartment, I'd confronted him. He'd begged me not to tell anyone and especially not the police. This had been enough for me to leave him. And this one night when I'd been alone in the apartment and had been packing my things, someone broke into our apartment."

The memories surged into my mind and tried to drag me down with them.

Jaro seemed to notice my struggle and put his hand on mine.

He did not urge me to continue, but since I had already started I wanted to follow through.

"I had been massively injured and left bleeding. At first, Sid had taken loving care of me. I'd thought that would mean the turn in our relationship, so I'd given him a second chance, but that was just a dream. It hadn't been two weeks before he'd started inviting shady people over again. When I'd said I was going to leave him for good this time, he'd beaten the crap out of me, saying, "What had worked once can work a second time." From that moment on, I'd known he'd staged the break-in. He had threatened to keep chasing me and beating me or give me to his trafficking friends even if I moved out."

I took a long breath.

Jaro drew lazy circles with his thumb on the back of my hand, soothing the shivers that ran through my body.

He did not dare to speak a word in fear of silencing me.

"After two years and countless abuse, I'd could hardly stand it. One evening, he'd came home and had been furious. Apparently, a deal had fallen through for him and, as usual, I'd been the resource of all the evil that befell him. He'd strangled me and... I guess the rest; you already know. I'd confessed to everything at the hospital and also made a report. I'd gave them all the names I had picked up. You know what was funny that night? Several times a glaring light had flown by the window when Sid had sat on me and..."

Invisible hands wrapped tightly around my neck.

My voice broke too painful and real the memory of that evening.

"You don't need to keep talking about it."

"It's ok. Here we are, a day before the trial and the scumbag and his people still manage to intimidate me." I replied with an attempted smile

Relief filled me. It had helped to tell him. Knowing he was here with me... *strange.*

I could see the indecision in his gaze, weighing his next words.

"Maybe you should get some help to figure this whole—"

"Stop it! I'm not some broken doll who needs help." I jumped up, dragging my hand from his.

"Calm down, that's not what I meant at all..." He wrung his hands.

"You don't need to tell me to calm down. I am calm. Very much so." I yelled.

I ran into my room and locked the door.

Jaro knocked on it.

"Back off."

Too great the shame of being seen as sick and fragile enough to crack into a million pieces.

I wasn't the one who needed help, but Sid.

CHAPTER TEN

"Please rise, Judge Kroldrath is coming." said the bailiff standing in front of the judge's desk.

It was hardly a table where the judge would sit.

In the gray tinged courtroom was a single chair in the middle, set lower under two rows of other chairs.

The chair in the center was made of solid mahogany wood, as well as the judge's bench that sat in front of it.

The other chairs themselves, which were also made of wood, stone or other materials, were covered with thick velvet cushions, and each had a different size and shape.

This was my first time in court and a kind of awe had gripped me the moment I'd arrived in front of the courthouse.

It was a huge black complex standing on scorched ground. The only spot in our city I knew that was not green and alive.

At the entrance hung a massive memorial plaque.

You shall not forget what once was. Together, all crea-

tures of this earth judge what is right and what is wrong.

I ROSE FROM MY CHAIR, A SHIVER RUNNING DOWN MY SPINE AS I watched the judge enter the room. Judge Cal Kroldrath, a half-orc, born of an orc and a human, the perfect combination to preside over the court, it appeared to me.

With him, eight other figures, dressed in black robes, entered the hall. Among them, I could make out some human and halfling. Mixed in between were monsters. Monsters that I did not know and that aroused feelings in me I did not want to go into. I lowered my gaze.

"Sit down." the entire room sank back into their chairs. The people behind Kroldrath had positioned themselves above him in the two rows of chairs. One of them had wings, which he had placed in the specially made recesses. Another had dipped his hands in bowls that were lost in blackness.

"I hereby open the hearing. This is a court formed of all the creatures this world houses. I, as the chairman of this court, will preside over this gathering. But do not be subject to the thought that my fellow judges will not also be watching every move and voicing their concerns." His heavy gaze slid around the room. I was allowed to take a seat in the audience and follow the proceedings until I had to testify myself.

"I may note all the invited parties, and I now call the defendant Sid Morgan to the stand."

Sid, whom I had ignored up to this point, rose and was led by a bailiff to the center of the room. There, he took a seat on a simple chair and his hands were tied to the table in front of him.

Tension rose in me and mixed with the shame I had felt all morning, threatened to flip my stomach.

I had woken after another night of bad rest.

I'd realized I needed to apologize to Jaro for my outburst. He had offered me help and was probably the first one to do so. At least the first genuine offer. I couldn't expect him to take this burden up on himself and being my therapist when there were professionals for this job.

I'd been so fucking stupid.

I looked over at Jaro, who was standing at one exit. I didn't know what role he would play today. Was he just there to assist the court in its task, or would he make a statement after working on my case?

This morning, after I'd finished washing up, I'd entered the kitchen on the hunt for him, but the only thing I'd found was a letter.

A letter I'd held on to since, like a ripcord that had been thrown to me when I was about to drown.

Dear Kaida,

The proceedings should be over today after the main hearing. So it should be safe for you to live alone again. I checked with the authorities and they assured me that they had found the person who had threatened you.

Sorry that I had you disturbed over this.

I'm sorry.

Jaro.

I ought not to let it go that far, I was not ready to be sent away like that.

Without me saying sorry or an explanation why he wanted me to vanish so quickly.

65

Was he done playing with me and wanted to throw this damaged doll out as soon as possible? Had he gotten what he wanted?

My hands curled around the paper.

Lost in thought, I didn't hear the part where Sid was questioned about his personal information and prosecutor Levana Blackbourne read the charges. I knew the points, trafficking, dealing in narcotics and finally the abuse of me.

"Mister Morgan, would you like to comment on the charges?"

Sid glanced at his attorney and then turned to me. His icy stare struck me to the core. Never had I seen such hatred, not even close to the way he had looked at me at the worst moments.

A filthy smile appeared on his face.

"Thank you, but I have nothing to say after being innocently denounced by that crazy chick."

A rumbling went through the courtroom, and I could feel a dozen eyes on me.

"Mister Morgan, I forbid myself such obscenities." admonished Judge Kroldrath, and asked the courtroom to be quiet.

"Since you have nothing to say, you can go back to your spot and we can start with the collection of evidence."

A woman behind Judge Kroldrath leaned down to him and whispered something in his ear. He nodded and his gaze sought mine.

"Miss Whyte, please come to the stand."

It happened way too fast. I didn't expect my appearance that early.

I stood up and straightened my shoulder, and shoved Jaro's letter into my pocket.

On my way to the front, I not once looked at Sid. I

remained focused on Jaro's face, the only familiar one in this room, hoping to drop an anchor.

I had to make him understand that I appreciated his help.

He stood confident and erect in his uniform, never letting his gaze stray from the spot on the window front across the room.

This should be the luckiest day for me. I would get the money I needed to start new and still I was unsettled.

I took my seat on the stand and smiled at the judges.

"Miss Whyte, first, please give me your personal information."

I did as asked of me and ended up with where I lived.

"Thank you very much. Since that is clarified. You know why you are here today?" the Judge asked.

"Yes, I know why I am here. I am supposed to give my statement regarding the actions of Mister Morgan. These include possession and trafficking of drugs, human trafficking and abuse."

"Exactly, that's what Mister Morgan is on the dock for here today. Since you are well informed, I give the floor to the prosecutor, Blackbourne. She will ask you a few questions." He said and nodded to Levana.

"Kaida, it's good to see you, doing well. I would like to ask you to share as much as possible with us today. We've all read your complaint and related testimony, but we'd like to reiterate some questions in court." She said, raising from her desk and coming into the center.

"Sure." I said.

"You have stated that you'd witnessed the acts of which Mister Morgan is accused. Is that correct?"

"Yes, that is correct. I had been in the adjacent room several times, supposedly asleep, or lying on the floor at his feet when he'd thought I had been unconscious."

67

I swallowed the lump in my throat.

"In the process, I could listen in on conversations that had talked about drop locations, types of drugs, races of people and monsters, and the like. There was also a lot of cash exchanged during many of the meetings."

"Was it ever said what purpose the humans or monsters were traded for?" Levana asked.

"No." That had been kept in the dark and only transferred via papers. I hadn't dared let my mind wonder to this question, ever.

"Thank you, that's enough." She nodded. "The abuse by Mister Morgan could be clearly documented on the day of your report, so there is no need for you to give us details. But allow me to ask, what ultimately led you to report him after two years?"

I sucked a deep breath into my lungs, trying to take in the experiences of that evening only from a distance.

"Actually, I had been lucky. If the two officers hadn't shown up that night of my report, I suspect I wouldn't be sitting here today. With the fake robbery, he had me practically broken and in his hands. I could not imagine ever taking that step. Never. My fear was too great." My voice trembled and a tear stole from my eye.

Levana came up to me and handed me a handkerchief. Not for a minute of my telling had I looked away from the judges on the bench. I could not live with seeing the looks of the spectators, Jaros and even Sids.

The broken doll who couldn't get her life together.

"So it had only because the officers had freed you from that hell that day?"

"Exactly, that was the only reason and probably the adrenaline that had made me get my courage up and finally turn Mister Morgan in. If he had just taken me to the hospital by himself and pulled the stair fall act again, I wouldn't had said anything."

"Then I'm glad you're here today and mustered the courage back then." A genuine smile appeared on her face.

"I thank you for your testimony." She turned to the bench. "I am through with my questions and convinced of the truth of the words Miss Whyte spoke to us today."

"Thank you very much, Miss Prosecutor, but that remains for the court to evaluate." The judge turned from her to the defendant's bench. "Counsel for the defense, you're on."

The defender was human and wore a bright red suit. Sid would never have let himself be defended by a monster, even if his chances were better. He made them work for him, like the dirt under his shoes.

The red suit stepped close to the table and propped one arm on it.

"Miss Whyte, we are all so glad to see you safe and sound here today." He laughed and let his gaze wander around the room. "But allow me to say how fantastically quickly you have recovered." His glazed face already pissed me off. "Do you really think we sit here and believe you just because you shed a tear?"

"I'm not here to proselytize anyone. I'm speaking the truth before this high court." I said, my pulse quickened. I reached into my pocket and clutched the letter inside.

"Commendable, but tell me, who's to say you weren't involved in this whole thing instead of just sleeping?"

"Pfft." I laughed.

"You don't need to laugh. Let me introduce you to my theory." With that, he turned to the judicial bench and looked everyone on it deeply in the eye.

"I think it was like this. You had worked with my client for a long time. You'd shared profits and had lived happily and abundantly for a long time. But one day you couldn't get enough and had attacked my client to get him out of the way." He paused for a long minute to let the thought sink in with the judges and audience in the room.

He turned back to me and lowered his voice a bit. "But my client had fought back that night. Which would also explain the injuries on your body. Wasn't it? " he asked.

"No, it wasn't like that."

"Then let me continue my theory." he paced back and forth in front of the table.

"So when you had been picked up by the police, you were happy not to die. This fact remains the same. But you knew the police would uncover everything now. That's why you had used this brilliant chance to falsely accuse my client and save your own skin. By the way, you put some of your competitors out of business with your testimony. What you were waiting for now was the trial, the conviction of Mister Morgan, the check that would be paid to you, and then you could start your new life."

"No, that's not true." Anger seeped through my voice.

"Then you'll have to explain to me why my team and I have been able to find travel and house brochures with you?"

My fist closed around the paper in my pants. My breath had quickened. I had enough of these pompous guys who thought they could trample over me.

I could take no more.

"First of all, what kind of absolute shit is this that a lawyer gets to go through my personal stuff?" I cast a scathing glance toward the bench.

"Dear court, I really respect you and your work, but this - please excuse my statement now - worm is a disgrace." Pointing my finger to red suit.

I rose from my chair and took a deep breath.

"Second, I wouldn't have to justify myself at all. But for fuck's sake. Yes, I have been waiting for this check since the day I made the report. Why? Because I'm a greedy woman. There's your statement. The rest you can get from the evaluation I had to undergo. You lunatic."

With that, I dropped back into my chair.

No sound could be heard, except for my rasping breath and probably my heart.

Tears stung my eyes, that I forced to stay inside.

"Are you done, Miss Whyte?" he turned to the judges. "And just that, very honorable court, shows the extent—"

The judge's gavel thundered through the courtroom.

"You should realize the magnitude of your investigation and work. Enough is enough. I will impose an administrative fine on you and also on you, Miss Whyte, for disturbing the peace of the court. And you can sit down." The red suit left the center of the court without another reaction, tail tucked in tightly.

"Anybody else have questions for Miss Whyte?" No one in the room spoke up or even dared to cough.

"Fine, then you' re dismissed and can take a seat in the back. Anything further concerning her person and testimony can be taken from the reports."

I stood up and hesitated for a moment as I passed Jaro. His gaze still fixed on nothing.

In front of me, Sid jumped off his bench. "You stupid bitch, just wait until I'll come out. I'll going to beat you so bad. You're not worth more than a punching bag." His words bounced off me.

Jaro took a leap forward and pushed him face down on the table. Briefly, his eyes darted to me, holding nothing but regret.

"Fuck your regret." I mouthed without making a sound. I expected him to understand me like that.

His gaze turned icy.

The message arrived.

I didn't need his regret. Hadn't he learned?

After the judge called Sid and the people in court to order, Jaro was called to the stand, which clarified my question. But I was not sure what he could contribute.

His details were also taken, and Levana stepped in front of him at the table.

"Officer Bishop, it was you who had worked intensively on the case surrounding Mister Morgan. Please let me and the court know how long you had been doing this?"

"I was ordered by my boss about two years ago to monitor apartment number two on Rose Street."

"Could you also describe for us what your tasks were and what you'd found out?"

"Of course. My job had been to shadow the apartment of Mister Morgan and look for anything unusual. Mister Morgan had previously stood out in some records."

I did not know.

"I could ultimately confirm through the testimony of Miss Whyte that the named individuals were in and out of the apartment regularly."

"Have you ever been able to listen in on conversations during that time?"

"No, that was not possible for me. Getting any closer would had jeopardized the mission because there were some higher-level criminals involved."

"And during all that time, had you ever notice Miss Whyte or the circumstances of her?"

"No, I'd never noticed. I'd merely shadowed the apartment at night, at the times when people also were coming and going. The fact that nothing was going on during the day was something another colleague could tell ahead of time. We knew about Mister Morgan's partner, but had no interest in her."

"Then what exactly was the job of the police if they never would have gotten any further information without Miss Whyte's report? Just watch the apartment and then what?"

"I'm afraid I don't know. It's not within my purview to concern myself with such questions. I had gathered information and pictures. Further pursuit of other subjects was the responsibility of other colleagues."

"Then how do you explain that on the night he'd abused her, of all nights, colleagues of yours had ringed the doorbell?"

I leaned forward.

"I..." He stopped.

"Please, Officer Bishop, tell me and the court how the rescue of Miss Whyte came about? Don't make us lose faith in the police?"

"It was me who had called my colleagues."

"How so?" Levana asked.

"As usual, I'd watched the apartment and witnessed the act that Miss Whyte had brought to the police's attention."

"I'll ask again. Was this the first time you had seen Miss Whyte in such a situation?"

The seconds ticked by with no response from Jaro.

"Officer Bishop, please answer the question." Judge Kroldrath said.

His shoulders tensed under his jacket.

"No. This hadn't been the first time."

Everything inside me spun. The floor slipped out from under my feet and I let my head fall between my legs.

This couldn't be happening.

Never.

That was the police.

73

They would step in.

"And why didn't you intervene sooner?" The judge's voice thundered through the room.

"I reported the first incident I noticed to my boss. He'd given me instructions to take no further action."

The judge inquired about further questions by the lawyers, but none remained. All the more questions, however, remained in me.

"Thank you officer. Please return to your post."

I followed how Jaro went back to his place, not a single glance in my direction. His face a cold mask.

"I hereby close the hearing of evidence. Lawyers make your pleas."

Mister red suit tried everything to taunt me and my motives in front of the court again. His verdict, Sid, was not guilty.

Levana demanded the maximum sentence of 15 years. I admired her for the zeal with which she fought for justice, even dough I didn't like the methods she'd used on me before. But her craft and talent were outstanding.

With her last sentence, she gazed at me and closed her plea, visibly satisfied.

The judge tapped his gavel. "The court retires for deliberation. Resume in two hours."

CHAPTER ELEVEN

THIS WAS MY OPPORTUNITY TO TALK TO JARO. I JUMPED UP from my chair and went straight to him. He broke out of his professional stupor and looked at me blank.

"I need to talk to you." I said.

He grabbed my arm and pushed me a little to the side. Behind me, they led Sid past us through the door next to us.

"Did you hook up with the next one, bitch?" he had stopped besides us.

Jaro let go of my arm and jumped in front of Sid. He leaned forward and his lips moved close to his ear. I couldn't make out what he was saying to him, too loud the people moving from the hall.

Sid's features wreathed in a disgusting smile, the smile that showed a growing idea in him. It made me feel sick. He took one last look at me before pushing past Jaro and out the door.

"What did you say to him?" I asked, as he returned to my side.

"Unimportant. Come on, we shouldn't be talking here."

He took my hand in his, which shocked me, and pulled me out of the courtroom with him.

"Where are we going?"

Without looking back, he pulled me through the corridors of the court, my question unanswered.

We stopped in front of a large door bathed in red.

He looked around to all sides, knocked on the door, and waited for a response, which did not come.

He turned the knob, opened the door, and gestured for me to go ahead.

I frowned and silently doubted him.

He shook his head and gave me a smile of confidence.

Okay, let's do this. I needed to talk to him.

He wouldn't make me disappear in a courthouse or anything.

I laughed.

His hand laid on my shoulder, and he nudged me into the room. Behind me, he closed the door and stopped very close to my back.

We were no longer in the courthouse.

This had to be another part of the earth.

The room was dressed in red. The floor, the walls, and even the furniture. A giant bed, a sofa, chairs around a big table, and everything was stuffed with plants. The ceiling lamps that bathed everything in a warm light absorbed the poverty of windows. And it was almost unbearably warm in this room.

I turned to Jaro, his body, lingering over mine.

"Where are we?"

He laughed. "Let's put it this way, there are Exotics who work here and need a break from work every now and then. This is one of many rooms designed specifically for that. I don't know exactly which creature uses this room, but I know I like it too." The corner of his mouth lifted in seduction.

Walking backwards, I pushed further into the room,

76

away from him and his added warmth. He followed my every step. I was too aware of his closeness. The cold that had ran through my veins before liquefied with each of his steps.

Now or never, I would not get another opportunity.

"I'm sorry for the way I treated you last night. You didn't say anything wrong," I whispered.

There, that was out of the way.

"But..." and I reached into my pocket for the letter. "...why did you just run off this morning and left me this ridiculous letter?"

He snorted. "Is this letter really that ridiculous if you've been reaching for it all this time?" he said, pulling the paper from my hand.

"Fine, then don't. Then tell me why you were so distant?"

Why did I even ask? He wasn't interested in me, so I should be happy. I was only here to apologize and not leave any more scorched earth with a person who was in my life.

The back of my knees hit the bed and I turned away. "You know what? I don't even want to know anymore. I apologized. That's all I wanted."

I shouldn't embarrass myself any further here. Anyway, I was going to start a new life and after my testimony in court; I was probably confirming his view of me, a money hungry lowly employee that he could bend to his will.

I wasn't.

Or was I?

His hands closed around my shoulders, and his claws forced their way into the fabric of my blouse. The connection sent shock waves through both of us.

"Let me go, please." I whispered.

His hot breath hit my ear. "How could I?"

A shudder ran through my entire body, and I closed my eyes. His hands burned through my blouse.

I stepped aside. "I am not your plaything."

"You aren't, though."

I turned back to him. "Why had you decided to go against your boss's orders that one night? You had told me you'd never seen me before?"

He wrung his hands and lowered his eyes, shutting me out. "That's not important right now, and it is true. I'd never seen your face."

He anchored his gaze with mine, just a hint of the emotion he had felt a moment ago.

"What do YOU want from me, Kaida?" Black lust drowned the green in his eyes.

"Nothing. I want nothing from you." I assured him and myself. "I don't want you, not like this."

"Then why can I smell you, little dragon?"

He came closer to me. Desire wafted from his eyes into his body and sank into my skin as he touched my neck. His other hand steadied on my hip, grazing under my blouse with his clawed hand.

He growled close to my face, his canines protruding clearly from under his upper lip.

His lips settled on my neck. We both held our breath.

My mind went blank.

His hand creased up my hip and over the seam of my breast.

I moaned and my body melted in his grip.

Both hands roamed now freely over my body.

He had to bend down in order to spread more kisses on my neck.

"Please." I whimpered.

"Shhh. Not so fast, little dragon. I want to savor every moment, savor you."

My knees trembled.

He grabbed me under my butt and lifted me onto the plush sofa.

His tail thumped violently on the floor.

Under sleepy eyes, I took him in.

His skin glowed almost completely. His trouser hung sinfully low on his hips. I caught myself not being able to wait to see them fall.

A laugh shook his powerful torso. "There, there, not so greedy."

I closed my eyes, unable to lose myself further in his gaze.

His tail stroked the outside of my legs. He felt as soft as a feather. My body was already ablaze and melted further at the points where our bodies touched.

I drew in my breath when I felt his claws on my bare belly.

Tracing my exposed belly upwards he pushed my blouse up with his palm. Tracing my erected nipples through my bra.

My loud moan filled the room.

With that, he stroked the claw of his index finger under the rim hooked his fingers in and freed my breasts from their prison. "You are so beautiful."

He took my nipple between his lips and alternately licked and bit it before turning to my other breast.

His tail crept further up and shifted his caresses to my inner thighs. He stroked along my legs under my skirt until he bumped into my panties.

"So wet and ready already."

"Jaro, please..." I whimpered again. Without ceasing, he made love to my breasts. Skillfully, his tail pushed my panties aside and gently stroked the outside of my labia.

"I'm going to give you what you crave." And with that, he

opened my labia and bore into my entrance. Delicately advancing, he slid in and out.

"You're driving me crazy." he said. A rumble thundered through my torso.

"Look at me, Kaida." With difficulty, I opened my eyes. His gaze hit me right between the legs and just from that alone, I could have come.

He leaned his forehead against mine.

"You are going to look me in the eye right now and by no means close those beautiful blue googly eyes. I want to see you."

My breath came in bursts. The tip of his tail swelled inside me and he continued rubbing me deeply. His left hand slid to my center and stroked my clit.

"That's right. Let yourself go."

He intensified his movements, and I felt the release rolling in like waves breaking on the beach.

"You'll tell me as soon as you want to come, beautiful."

I swallowed hard and nodded toward him.

"Jaro."

"What do you want? Tell me."

"I want to come."

"Then come my beauty." he said.

The tip of his tail rode me hard, and it twitched with each successive stroke.

My toes tightened, and an explosion formed inside me.

"Keep your eyes open." he growled back at me. Only with difficulty could I keep my lids open, but his probing gaze only intensified my ride.

He moaned loudly in front of me and I couldn't hold on either. His tail twitched.

"Damn." he groaned out between clenched teeth. "You're so good."

He rested his head on my chest, and we breathed heavily into each other.

His tail pulled out of me, caressing.

He looked at me, and his lips settled on mine. We both held our breath taking in the situation.

Neither pulled back, spurring him to take my lower lip between his and nibble on it.

The situation hit me full force.

I pushed him off me and tumbled from the sofa and to the door.

"I can't do this."

CHAPTER TWELVE

I BLEW THE AIR BETWEEN MY LIPS TO SCARE AWAY THE LOOSE strands of my fringe.

The trial would continue at any moment, but there was no sign of Jaro. My hands clenched in my lap.

I had blown it.

No, I had done the right thing.

The thing with Jaro was wrong. A man like him didn't suit me.

Liar.

I squeezed my eyes shut to hold back the tears.

"All rise!" the bailiff's voice boomed through the courtroom.

For the last time, the hall stood up in unison. The judges entered the room. The last to follow was the chairman, a cream-colored folder in his hand. It contained my future.

My heart beat slow and loud in my chest. Judge Kroldrath took his seat in the middle of the bench. He let his gaze wander.

Determined, he flipped open the folder.

"The court has agreed on a verdict after a long deliberation. The sentence is passed in the name of the new world.

We sentence Sid Morgan to a term of 15 years in a labor camp."

My heart slipped into the pit of my stomach. I had to brace myself on my knees.

Sid cried out, and the guards were already holding him in place.

Jaro was one of them. I hadn't noticed that he had returned to the room.

There was no trace of what had happened before.

"Mister Morgan, sit down and be quiet." Kroldrath banged his gavel. "You may sit. Let me continue with the reasoning." He waited another moment until everyone had quieted down. "We are convinced of your guilt and the crimes you have committed against the people and creatures of this world. In addition, some of your associates have been blabbing to mitigate their own punishment. These will remain anonymous in these proceedings, but rest assured, everyone will get their just punishment."

Tears stole from my eyes. It was over. Finally.

I did not care that I would not receive any money.

Judge Kroldrath continued. "15 years is the norm for the sentence. What is unusual is the way. You are a disgrace to this planet and have made other beings work for you and treated them like dirt. We will not treat you like that. But you will make parts of our world habitable again with you labor in the camp and thus contribute. You will not be applauded for this. Further, the only aggrieved party located, Miss Whyte, will receive compensation of three million Ethereal Coins."

What?

My gaze darted to the bench.

This was way too much.

The judge nodded at me.

I could barely hold myself together. My arms closed around my upper body.

From a distance, I could hear the fading of the bustle that had set in after Judge Kroldrath had ended the hearing.

I was still sitting on the chair with my arms clasped and my head between my knees.

I could not believe it.

I had done it.

Sid would never be able to hurt me again.

I just let the tears flow.

"Kaida." Someone touched my back.

Everything felt so heavy, but I pushed my body up against the gloom.

"Hi." Levana said with a smile on her lips. "Can I give you a ride home?"

I shook my head, and she sat down next to me.

"Aren't you supposed to be celebrating?"

I wiped away the tears with the back of my hand. "Probably. But I don't feel like it right now."

She laughed. "Then let me tell you this. Think about what others have sacrificed for you here today."

"What?" I looked at her in disbelief.

"Officer Bishop, well Jaro... he didn't have to save you."

"Then why the hell did he?"

"I can't answer that. I just know he risked his job to do it. As of the end of today, he's suspended. Whether they'll hire him back remains to be seen."

Never.

No one would do that for a stranger, and certainly not Jaro.

"Think about it." She stood up and left the court, clacking.

He'd told me he had never seen the woman, me, before, which made me a stranger. And yet he had helped me.

Why?

That did not fit into the picture I had of him.

Wrong.

Damn, I'd screwed up.

This sentence kept echoing through my head, besides the other things I called myself.

Why had I pushed Jaro away from me when he was the one helping me?

He had made me feel myself again, from the beginning.

He had never forced himself on me.

What we just did was great, but the kiss marked the end for me?

I had seen what happened when I let people in, they, they...

They were hurting me.

Yeah, right, they definitely did.

Liar.

I dropped my head on the back of the chair in my back.

What had Jaro really did to me?

He hadn't said that I was mentally broken and therefore needed help. I apologized for my behavior, but had I forgiven him for his statement?

No. Because I was too afraid of what would come afterwards. What would happen if I forgave a person.

I had to find out.

For me.

For him.

For a possibility of us.

I just wasn't sure if my brain and heart were blinded by hormones or if I had something real in my hands.

Bu I needed to find out.

CHAPTER THIRTEEN

I ANNOYED MYSELF.

But not because of Jaro. There was no reason to be angry with him or push him away like that.

I had everything in my hands to start a new life and find the first real relationship in my life. To perhaps find someone for whom I came first and who equally longed for the things I did for myself.

I knocked at his door and waited.

Nothing.

I couldn't just go home now.

I pushed down the handle and the door opened, it was unlocked.

"Jaro?" My voice echoed from the walls of his hallway.

No answer.

I opened the door a little more and saw the open door to the roof terrace.

I went inside and closed the door behind me, walking up the stairs to the roof, my ears pricked for any noise.

But nothing.

Maybe he was just not home and had forgotten to lock his door. Which seemed unusual for a policeman.

A calm breeze and the night sky full of stars greeted me when I stepped out the second door. I turned to the swing seat, but he was not there either, only a book was lying on it with its spine up.

I went to the edge of the roof where I had been sitting and had fallen when he tried to kiss me. I am sometimes just so stupid.

A thud vibrated from the floor through my body. I scooted around and in front of me was Jaro, shirtless, with his wings slowly retracting.

"Hi," I said and lowered my head.

He laughed.

My gaze shot to him. "Why are you laughing?"

"Nothing. You're just... forget it. What brings you here?" he asked.

I took a deep breath and braced myself for my speech. "Please, let me finish speaking first."

"Sure." His hands splayed loosely in front of his chest, which made it hard for me to fully concentrate.

"I wanted to apologize. It was stupid that I'd just taken off." I was breathless. "It had been about me. Everything had overwhelmed me, with the trial, the threats, you, the kiss and us..."

"I noticed that." He smiled at me.

"I could not forgive you for the help you obviously wanted to give. Even if there was nothing to forgive, but inside me.... I do not know."

"Kaida, look at me." he said, lifting my chin to him. "There's nothing to apologize for. Earlier was just wonderful and I thank you for the gift. I hope you did not feel taken advantage of. I knew I had screwed up and swore not to approach you again."

"Yes there is. I wanted to apologize for not giving us a chance, even though I don't know what that is between us.

For not trusting you. For stopping myself from experiencing this." I showed between us, reaching out and tried to kiss him. Making the first move this time.

He pulled away.

Damn, I had messed up.

"Before we continue, there is something I wanted to show you." he said.

"Show?"

"Do you trust me?" he asked.

"I'll try."

"Thats good enough for me."

Before my eyes, he dissolved into a glistening ball of light. I wrenched my hands up to shield my eyes.

"What are you doing?" the light vanished and in front of me stood the dragon I had seen only once in front of the police station.

Goosebumps ran down my spine.

He was the dragon that had saved me that night.

It could only be this dragon. Never would there be a second of this kind. Even though I knew nothing about dragons. This one was special, because of the drawing of its scales, dipped in purple and green.

I pushed past the fear and stepped closer, caressing the side of his face. The contact ignited a storm in me. "Jaro? Is this really you?"

The dragon wheezed.

"Thank you." I kissed him on his broad muzzle.

In his eyes, I could see Jaro raising his eyebrow.

He shook himself and bent down to me with one side, tucking his wing close to his body.

"You're not really asking me to get on your back, are you?" A whip of his tail told me to do just that. "I must be crazy." And climbed onto his back. "I hope I'm not hurting you or too heavy."

88

A snort left his big muzzle and, without warning, we took off toward the sky.

I screamed and slammed forward to grab onto his horns. Without thinking about potentially hurting myself. But I knew I could trust Jaro at this point. He would do nothing that could harm me.

He was a dragon that could have easily hurt or killed me. In his Drakon form and in this form. But he didn't.

I took a deep breath and inhaled the fresh night air. I didn't mind the cold because Jaro was my personal heating pad.

I enjoyed every second.

After some time, I felt safe and let go of his horns and stretched my arms.

I flew and a bubbling laugh wafted out of me.

He took a turn, which only made me laugh harder.

Jaro, on the other hand, snorted. My sign to behave civilized again and hold on tight. He went into the descent and flew towards a rock wall.

He's not going to fly us into it, is he?

I squinted my eyes.

But when we came closer, I saw a gap in the rock face. A bright light was coming from it.

Jaro was heading straight for it and maneuvered us into the entrance with no problems.

In front of me was a gigantic cave with small blue lights on the ceiling.

He sank further down and below us I could make out a lake into which he was now heading.

I screamed, but in the next moment, the water masses buried my scream.

I opened my eyes, and the large glowing ball appeared again in the water. Jaro appeared in front of me and pulled me up with him.

I gasped for air. "Where are we?" I asked in amazement.

"This, my little dragon, is the White Shallow cave. My cave."

"You own a cave?"

"I own quite a bit, but it doesn't matter now. Come on my back."

I clung to him, and with me he swam to a less deeper part of the lake.

The water reflected the blue light of the ceiling. A warmth clung to my body.

He set me down and turned to face me.

His lips rested on mine, and a moan escaped him.

"God how I missed this." He said, leaning his forehead against mine.

"Wait a minute, you missed this?" I pointed between the two of us.

"Yes."

"But we kissed only once, and it was maybe like 10 hours ago."

"It doesn't matter." He laughed and lifted my face with his claw under my chin.

He put his lips on mine again. The initially tender kiss became more and more urgent. "I want to show you that you are worth so much."

I shuddered.

His tail wrapped around my leg and nuzzled my butt. His lips kissed their way down from my jaw to my neck. His canines nibbled at my skin.

A whimper came from my lips.

"Are you ready for me already?" he asked.

His hands got rid of my cardigan. I clawed at his bare shoulders to keep my grip.

With his claws, he cut the straps of my top. In the middle

of my bra he started again and with a jerk my upper body was naked.

He took a step back. "I will never be able to get enough of you, my little dragon."

He bent down and took my nipples one by one in his mouth and caressed them, first tenderly, then fiercely.

He let his hands slide down, shredding my skirt in the next moment.

I took my panties off.

He grabbed my wrist and pulled my hand with my panties in to his nose.

Sniffing.

Inhaling deep.

He pressed my fingers into his mouth, licking the lacy material. A gut-clenching groan escaped him. He bit the pantie from my hand and leaned down to undress himself.

My panties still hung sinfully on his plump lips.

We both stood naked and couldn't take our eyes off each other.

"Why does it glow under water?" I said and dove.

I choked on the water and he helped me up. "Is that normal?"

He twisted his beautiful mouth into a crooked grin; the pantie gone.

"Yes, it's very normal. It's for reproduction purpose and I was once told it feels fantastic."

He looked me up and down and worked himself, his hand wrapped with my panties. The glow intensified.

"Interested?" he asked.

I jumped at him and slung my arms and legs around him. Leaning down on him, tasting the sweetness of me in his mouth. He raked the fingers of his other hand that did not pleasure himself through my wet-soaking hair and opened his mouth so wide for me that I poured everything into him. Every inch of my past and the gratitude for a future with him.

I tilted my head and stroked my tongue with his. He moaned deep into me. Giving me everything he had, leaving us both raw and open to be seen.

His hand left his cock and grabbed my butt. He pressed me further down and kissed me deeper, harder, relentlessly than anyone before did. Erasing everything from before. A clean plate for him to dirty, lighten, darken, paint, bite and use.

I needed this.

We gripped for the other, for every contact of skin we could get.

His claws scraped over my skin, but did not open me.

Pushing me further down, splaying me wide over his stomach, both hands landed on my butt, raking along my back.

My nipples rubbed against his broad, scale-covered chest, electrifying my insides.

His dick rocked against my sex whenever he kneaded my butt with his calluses hands.

My hands switched from grasping his hair to trying to reach his cock from between our body. But he pressed himself even tighter against me.

"Relax." He whispered in my ear, biting down on my earlobe.

My nails dug into his muscular arms.

His hips rocked higher, grazing my entrance as his mouth opened wider over mine. His tongue slick and savage.

His tail snaked around my leg again, working its way up, up ,up and in between my butt cheeks. I gasped for air, pulling it from his lungs.

He leaned back, taking his mouth from mine and looked at me.

"You have it in your hand. I'm doing nothing you don't want or are ready to give." His eyelids lowered in lustration.

This was not just about sex and satisfaction. It was about so much more. About claiming my body and my lust for myself.

I nodded, and he lowered his mouth to mine again and devoured me whole.

Two became one.

"I want you." His voice laced in every black of the night.

Not a question, a command.

Matching me.

I dropped and took him in me.

We stopped breathing.

All we could do was feel.

He was a wild monster that kept himself restrained. Viscous lust bubbling under the surface.

I took him deeper and my pussy clenched in sweet pain around him. My legs clasped around him.

And he broke.

He seated himself in me, filling me with his complete length.

I screamed.

Not from pain, but from incurable lust.

This was something I had never felt before.

His cock felt like nothing I had ever experienced.

He pulled out, and my core screamed in displeasure.

I needed him.

We shared a stare and he moved back inside me.

He withdrew, then thrust forward.

Hard and sharp.

Deep and possessing.

I scratched his bare arms. His tail still lingering between my cheeks, caressing my anus with feathery strokes.

He touched me everywhere, and it was still not enough.

I moaned into his mouth, and he snapped, leaving every control behind.

He thrust and thrust, grunting with each pass down his length.

His tail pushed into me from behind.

I cried out, my core pulsing dangerously. "You're not coming until I tell you. And fuck... I need to see your eyes when you do so."

His words alone pushed me close to the edge.

"I can't anymore." I begged.

"You will."

He bit down on my bottom lip, my blood mingling in with our tongues fighting.

Water was my bed and the warm air my sheets as I lost myself in him forever.

I dug my heels into the back of his thighs and rocked my hips with his movements.

My clit rubbed against the base of his cock. Tail stroking my insides. Sparks ignited behind my eyes and I tore them open.

"Oh god, please I need to come." I moaned.

My body tightened like a string, stretching with each stroke.

His mouth found my ear. His quickened breath revealing how lost he was.

"Come." Biting my earlobe.

This was my trigger.

The orgasm cracked me in half. Not just my core clenched, but my whole body.

It poured fire in my womb and blazed in fireworks down my pussy.

I came around his cock and tail.

I came like I had never had before.

His hips switched from fucking to impaling.

He took my gaze hostage, fucking me with his eyes. My core melting to no return.

He chased his own release, gripping me tight.

Growling deep inside me.

He grunted as his knees buckled, crashing his mouth to mine, feeding me his lust.

His cock and tail spurted in unison inside me, on and on.

This perfection sent me over the edge a second time. My pussy and ass sucking him dry.

He ensured I would never walk from him.

I was his.

And he was mine.

~

HE LIFTED ME UP INTO HIS ARMS AND LAID US BOTH DOWN ON the adjacent sandy beach. We gasped and tried to catch our breath again.

He leaned on his arm and laid his head down. With his other hand, he drew circles on my belly.

"Why have you saved me that night?" I asked.

"I had a dream the night before, about a woman with beautiful blue eyes. It had shaken me to the core. They were so full of sadness. I awoke from the dream that night and could not forget her." His eyes were full of sadness and anger. "That night when I saw what Sid was doing, I couldn't think of anything but those sad eyes. I'd had enough." He drew in a shaky breath.

"Then when I saw you for the first time in the bathhouse, the eyes found the face where they belonged. From that moment on, I was doomed."

"You'd painted those eyes?"

He nodded. "That brings me to the question. How do you know?" He tickled my belly.

"Stop!!! I took a brief tour of your apartment."

"That also explains why my room was full of your scent of cloves and wild yew." he said.

Which was the same scent that I'd used as an aroma for his massage. By his request.

Embarrassed, I narrowed my eyes. "The painting is beautiful, but also creepy."

"Thank you."

"Why did you become a cop?" I asked.

"Surely you can see how my skin glows. My kind is predestined for it. We track down bad guys and then shine a light on their houses. That way, our colleagues on the ground can organize arrests silently. At least, that's how it used to be, or something like it."

A laugh shook me.

"Hey don't laugh at me. I was originally supposed to become a healer. Maybe you noticed, but my light has the power to heal wounds faster. I don't have it under control, though, and it happens more by accident." He said, and his look became sad.

"I see. No matter what you are, I like you the way you are, especially your little shining friend." I raised an eyebrow.

"You beast, he's not little." He grumbled, tickling my belly again.

"Stop. Stop it, I surrender." I gave in while laughing.

"Good call my little dragon." he said and leaned in to kiss me.

"Why do you call me little dragon?" Puzzled, he looked

96

at me and flicked my nose. "Your name means little dragon. Didn't you know that, silly? It was faith that we met."

"No, how could I—"

"Enough with the chatter." He sealed my lips with his. And I knew exactly why he wanted to end our conversation. His cock was once again in full bloom, illuminating the space between our bodies.

"One more thing." I said, pushing him off me. "How good is your nose, and is it normal that you always give off such a scent?"

Blush crept into his cheeks. With downcast eyes he replied, "I can smell very well if you mean the day you had satisfied yourself? True, I could smell your arousal. As well as every other day that you had pined for me. Even if I had not wanted to admit it at first. And yes, as soon as I see a woman I like, my body sends out scents to lure her."

"You scoundrel!" I slapped him on the shoulder. Now it was my turn to blush.

"Hey, that hurt."

"I'm sure it did." I said.

"Now my turn: Were you thinking of me when you satisfied yourself?"

"Who knows?" I smiled and sealed my lips.

"You are the monster in this relationship, and I think you have something to make up for, trespassing into my bedroom when I haven't seen yours yet."

"You're sure of that?" I asked and braced myself on my arms and pushed him all the way down into the sand.

"What are you doing?"

"Shut up." I sealed his lips with my mouth and bit his lower lip. His claws ran tenderly over my back.

I spread my kisses down, down, down.

It would be the first time I could take his cock into full account.

I traced the thick veins running the length of his shaft with my index finger. He shuddered under me.

"This is my playtime, and you will tell me when you want to come."

His eyes widened, but a delicious smile spread across his mouth.

He liberated me.

The light intensified with every touch I brought down on him. His tail thumping next to me.

I reached out my hand and grabbed him. He flinched.

"What are you doing?" A nervous laughter escaped him.

"Since you won't tell me exactly what your tail is all about, I'll just have to explore it myself."

And that's what I did by gently wrapping my fingers around the end of his tail, which was shaped like a diamond, and squeezing it tightly.

A growl escaped him. "You're driving me crazy."

Spurred on by his praise, I lowered my head into his lap and licked the thick head of his glans with the tip of my tongue.

Pre cum emerged from his slit, leaving a salty, full taste on my tongue.

His hands clenched and unclenched next to him, and I knew this was costing him all his strength. But he gave me his trust and I would reward him for it.

I let my hand slide up and down around his tail. The shape changed to an elongated rhombus and swelled.

After licking up and down his shaft and tasting every part of his skin, I took the complete length of him in my mouth. He was huge and also filled my mouth. I moaned and moisture ran down my thighs.

Perfect.

I pressed my mouth together and created a pull. With

my hand I worked his tail faster and with the other hand I worked his heavy testicles.

With each deep thrust in my mouth, my nose pressed into his belly and I inhaled his wonderful aroma of citrus and mountains dew.

He went mad under me and his claws lengthened and dug violently into the sand.

My darkness sprang onto him, and with each up and down, I took his darkness into me.

I released his cock and took the tip of his tail in my mouth.

If he was shaped almost exactly like a penis and could also swell and spray a liquid when he came, then it would probably feel just as good.

"FUUUCK." he screamed, confirming my theory.

His hands shot into my hair, and his claws tingled on my scalp. His hips thrust upward and his penis buried itself slick between my breasts.

Jackpot.

"If you keep going, I will come in the next second." He kept thrusting, growling.

I released his tail. "I want you to come on my tongue. Your tail..." I let the words hang in the air and replaced his penis between my breasts with his tail. His penis I took back into my mouth. I felt the power he willingly gave me shoot through me, increasing the high I was on.

Up and down, up and down.

He continued to swell. The light that emanated from him almost blinded me.

His tail rubbed wildly and wetly between my breasts.

I pressed my legs together, providing friction.

"I want to come." he said.

I smiled around his cock and laced my tongue around his big head.

Sucking and biting down.

His hips thrust upward and met my mouth halfway.

I nodded, and he let go.

One more lick from my mouth and he spurted into me. Filling my mouth.

His tail rode between my breast.

I moaned with him in unison. From this view alone, I could come.

His tail slipped down from my breasts and buried itself inside me.

I couldn't stop the sudden orgasm, running towards me. I took my hand and rubbed my core. With the other hand, I kneaded his testicles to get every drop from him.

My mouth sucked him and my pussy his tail dry.

I collapsed over him. His heavy length on his belly.

His pungent juice ran from the corner of my mouth and he smudged the trail with his thumb and licked it off.

My eyes grew huge.

"Thank you, little dragon."

I smiled. "Thank you." And winked at him.

Coming was the easiest thing in the world with him. I only had to look at him, and I was already ready again.

With him, it wasn't just sex, that much I was sure of. With him, it would become so much more.

He made me whole.

STAY IN TOUCH

Did you like the book? I would be very happy about a review on Amazon.

**Release Day Alerts, Sneak Peek
and Newsletter**
To be first to know about upcoming releases, please join Edith's Newsletter.
https://subscribepage.io/edithsada_newsletter

For more, scan the QR-Code at the back of this book.

ACKNOWLEDGMENTS

Thank you to my amazing friend, partner in crime, listener,
twin soul and all the things I could think of.
Thanks to my husband who let me spend all the weekends
on my dream without complaining.
Thanks to you, the reader, for giving this book and the
„heroes" of the story a chance.
Edith